MW01490438

MURDER ON MALLOWAN COURT

A GINGER GOLD MYSTERY BOOK 17

LEE STRAUSS

la plume
PRESS

Copyright © 2021 by Lee Strauss - All rights reserved.

Cover by Steven Novak, Illustrations by Tasia Strauss

No part of this book may be reproduced in any form or by any electronic or mechanical means, including information storage and retrieval systems, without written permission from the author, except for the use of brief quotations in a book review.

Library and Archives Canada Cataloguing in Publication

Title: Murder on Mallowan Court / Lee Strauss.

Names: Strauss, Lee (Novelist), author.

Series: Strauss, Lee (Novelist). Ginger Gold mystery; 17.

Description: Series statement: A Ginger Gold mystery; 17 | "A 1920s cozy historical mystery."

Identifiers: Canadiana (print) 20210194901 | Canadiana (ebook) 2021019491X | ISBN 9781774091654 (hardcover) | ISBN 9781774091647 (softcover) | ISBN 9781774091685 (IngramSpark softcover) | ISBN 9781774091678 (Kindle) | ISBN 9781774091661 (EPUB)

Classification: LCC PS8637.T739 M96 2021 | DDC C813/.6—dc23

GINGER GOLD MYSTERIES
(IN ORDER)

*M*rs. Ginger Reed, known by some as Lady Gold, was in her study at Hartigan House in South Kensington. Her focus was on the door that had just closed with a decided click behind another nanny applicant she'd dismissed that day. This one was too fastidious. The others were either too simple or too ambitious. A nanny for her child should possess a balance of all the virtues: patient yet firm, jovial yet serious, experienced but not set in her ways. The perfect candidate must be a good fit for the family and current staff at Hartigan House, one who got along with others while standing up for herself if need be. She must have some education and be well spoken, as the child would take a lot of his or her speaking cues from the care taker.

The tightening sensations gripped her once again,

and she cupped her protruding stomach as if holding on would make the discomfort dissipate. She breathed slowly through her nose the way her friend Matilda Hill, a vicar's wife and a knowledgeable midwife, had instructed her to.

Ginger's doctor, Dr. Longden, assured her that these were not actual labour pains but practice contractions, coined Braxton Hicks after the English physician who had first described them. With two weeks before a safe delivery could be assured, Ginger took little comfort in Dr. Braxton Hicks' discovery and wondered if she would know the difference when real labour began.

The next nanny wouldn't be arriving to be interviewed until after teatime, and Ginger was quite ready for a good cup of tea. Bracing herself against the armrests of her leather desk-chair, Ginger stood, resting one hand on her lower back for good measure. The first two trimesters of her pregnancy seemed to have flown by, but this last one was dragging like a directionless slug. She wanted to continue carrying the babe inside for the child's sake, but her own body and frame of mind wanted the ordeal to be over with.

For one thing, Ginger couldn't wait to go back to donning proper dresses. Glancing down at the layered, "handkerchief-style" frock she wore, with well-placed, irregular flounces draped diagonally and made from a bold floral print that distracted the eye, Ginger dreamed of the new spring 1927 designs she and her seamstress at Feathers & Flair were working on. Modern styles were more slimming with straight cuts, pleated skirts, and shorter hemlines, favouring chiffon and silk fabrics ranging in colours from soft beige to deep purple. Ginger could hardly wait.

"Come on, Bossy." Ginger whistled softly to the little black-and-white Boston terrier sleeping in his bed at the foot of the fireplace, the embers glowing orange, warming the dismal November day. Her pet slowly uncurled himself, then followed her down the corridor to the sitting room, his claws making clicking noises on the marble floor.

Pippins, Ginger's long-time butler, a septuagenarian with a balding head and friendly cornflower-blue eyes, stood at the tall windows in the entrance hall, hands behind his back, shoulders stooped and looking out. He turned when he heard Ginger approaching.

"Madam," he said. "Are you ready for your tea?"

"Thank you, Pips. I'll take it in the sitting room." Her curiosity piqued, Ginger stepped to the window and stared across Mallowan Court.

"Lady Whitmore is moving away," he said.

Men in overalls were awkwardly carrying heavy

furniture out of the front entrance of Lady Whitmore's House and onto waiting lorries.

Ginger nibbled a lip. "I didn't realise Lady Whitmore's move was scheduled for today." She'd been so focused on finding a nanny that time had got away from her. Still, it bothered her that she'd let something like that slip.

"It was meant to happen next week," Pippins said, and Ginger felt reassured that pregnancy hadn't stripped her of her cognitive acuteness, at least not entirely.

Pippins continued, "Apparently, the new owners, a family called Foote, wanted to move in earlier than first reported."

Ginger's lips twitched with amusement. She, a celebrated private investigator, and her husband, Basil, a chief inspector at Scotland Yard, often came in second to her staff when it came to detecting neighbourhood gossip.

"I wanted to have Lady Whitmore over for tea before she left. I wonder, am I too late?"

Pippins stepped back. "Shall I ring Lady Whitmore and make an invitation on your behalf?"

"That would be splendid, Pips," Ginger said. "Thank you. And if she accepts, do let Lady Gold know so that she can join us."

The dowager Lady Gold, Ambrosia, was Ginger's

former grandmother-in-law and the grandmother of her late husband, Daniel. She had become a permanent guest at Hartigan House. Daniel's sister Felicia had resided with Ginger until her recent nuptials.

Ginger moved through the double doors that opened to the sitting room. Like the rest of the house, Ginger had redecorated it after she'd moved back in '23. She'd used soft lemon on the walls, sizeable jade Persian rugs on the wooden floors, rose-coloured, straight-lined armchairs, and matching settees and ottomans across from the fireplace on the outside wall. Tall windows facing the street let in lovely natural light.

Lowering herself into her favourite chair, she put her feet up on the ottoman and let out a long breath. Since the practice contractions had started, she'd been strongly admonished by Basil, Matilda, and Dr. Longden to dramatically reduce her schedule. That meant no more clients for Lady Gold Investigations or time on the floor of her dress shop, Feathers & Flair. Fortunately, she had competent staff and could manage her part by remaining at her office letter writing and making telephone calls. Still, she missed interacting with other people and driving her lovely Crossley through the streets of London.

While Felicia was away on her wedding journey, Ginger had struggled with a rare condition for her—

boredom. Felicia had only recently returned, and Ginger didn't expect to see much of her former sister-in-law for at least a few days, as Witt House, even grander than Hartigan House, would require much of her attention.

Tea with an elderly widow and her aged grandmother would be the most exciting thing to happen to her in days.

Her gaze landed on the John William Waterhouse painting that hung on the stone fireplace above the mantel. *The Mermaid* was a rather provocative piece of art, with a nearly nude mermaid perched on a rocky beach, her full and lengthy red locks protecting her modesty. The painting had been a gift from Ginger's father to her mother. Ginger had inherited her red hair from her mother, and it was a trait they both shared with the mythical mermaid.

Ginger had only a few photographs and a painted portrait to remember her mother by, as she had passed away only a few days after Ginger was born. Like Ginger, she had conceived late in life, and though her father had reassured her she wasn't to blame for her mother's death, Ginger could never quite accept that to be true.

And now, here she was, only a short time away from her own delivery experience. Would she survive it?

The baby kicked as if he or she wanted to knock Ginger out of her dark train of thought. Rubbing the imprint of the small foot that pressed against her stomach, Ginger whispered, "So long as you make it, little one."

Ginger had faced danger and tackled fear before, especially during the Great War when she'd worked for the British secret service, but she felt more fragile and out of control with her impending labour than she ever had during those years. Then, like now, it was about her own potential loss of life, but unlike now, her child's life had not been at stake.

She jumped at another sharp kick and laughed. "All right, Rosa. I'll stop the doom-and-gloom thinking."

She and Basil had agreed on the name George for a boy, after Ginger's late father, and Rosa for a girl, a tribute to the steamship, the SS *Rosa*, where they had met. The vessel was not only special due to it being the place where their friendship and relationship had begun, but it was where they had both first met their adopted son, Scout, a street "orphan" who'd worked in steerage at the time and had taken care of Boss.

The door between the sitting room and the dining room opened, and Grace, one of the household maids, pushed in the tea trolley. Three teacups and a plate of small sandwiches indicated that Lady

Whitmore and Ambrosia would be joining Ginger shortly.

"Good afternoon, madam," Grace said, then busied herself with setting the tea tray on the low table in front of the settee.

THE TAPPING sound of Ambrosia's walking stick alerted Ginger to the elderly lady's arrival. The dowager Lady Gold was caught between the centuries. On an impulse, she had had her traditional grey bun, which had been pinned loosely to the top of her head, chopped into a modern bob, a move she continued to regret. Still, the effort it would take to grow her hair long enough to tie into a bun was too much for the older lady to bear, so she reluctantly kept it short.

Ginger thought that the style was growing on her former grandmother-in-law, but Ambrosia wasn't the type to admit to that. Instead, she steadfastly wore her corset and her stiff upper lip, and though she allowed for a drop in the waist of her frock, she would never concede to a hemline that brushed her knees.

"Good afternoon," she said, taking the seat nearest Ginger. "I understand we're being honoured with a visit from Lady Whitmore. A final hurrah," she added dryly.

"Somehow, I doubt that," Ginger replied.

Ambrosia stiffened as she shot Ginger a haughty look. "One doesn't entertain for the sake of one's immediate neighbours."

Lady Whitmore had resumed her regular letters to the newspaper editor, giving her opinion and advice on various topics. However, because she was still officially in mourning after the death of her husband seven months earlier, she did so using a nom de plume.

Their guest arrived as if she'd mounted a small tornado to travel the short distance across the cul-de-sac. Her shrill voice echoed across the high ceilings of the entry hall.

"Oh, dear Pippins, how I will miss seeing you and all the family of Hartigan House. Do take my shawl, will you, but be careful with it. It's made of the finest cashmere India has on offer."

"Of course, my lady," Pippins returned. "Mrs. Reed and Lady Gold are waiting in the sitting room."

"Thank you. I can find my way." She tittered. "I've been here before, but it has been ages, hasn't it?"

Ginger got to her feet as the sitting room door opened. Pippins was rather red-faced, having raced up the stairs—Ginger imagined—to prevent their spry neighbour from announcing herself.

"Lady Whitmore," he said.

"Thank you, Pippins," Ginger said.

Her butler gave a nod of appreciation before stepping out. Ginger smiled warmly at Lady Whitmore, who was dressed in widow's black from head to toe. "Do have a seat, Lady Whitmore. I apologise for waiting until the last minute to invite you over, but I was under the impression that your planned departure was still weeks away."

Lady Whitmore settled on the far end of the settee and sniffed as she removed her gloves, one finger at a time. She'd aged since the passing of her husband, Lord Whitmore, who'd died in a rather scandalous fashion, and Ginger wasn't sure if the lady was in her fifties or sixties or beyond. Her mind remained quick, regardless.

"It's the Footes," Lady Whitmore said.

Ambrosia jutted her soft chin. "Surely you mean 'feet', Lady Whitmore."

"I assure you, I do not. 'Foote' with an *E*, is the surname of the family which has purchased Whitmore House. Oh dear, I suppose it won't be called that any longer." She turned her neck sharply to Ginger. "You're quite in the family way? Forgive me for being blunt, but it's hardly a secret."

Ginger patted her protruding stomach. "Not at all. However, I can still pour the tea." She reached for the teapot and drew one of the empty teacups and saucers closer. "Do help yourself to the sandwiches," she added. Mrs. Beasley, her cook, had cut the cucumber and salmon sandwiches into dainty, crust-free triangles.

"This Foote family," Ambrosia started, "how is it that they've come to inconvenience you so?"

Lady Whitmore lifted her chin. "Well, it was more of a mix-up on my part, I must confess." She sighed, suddenly looking masterfully forlorn. "Since my George died, I've just not been myself. And that house is simply too big for one person. I felt alone living in a massive cave."

With all her servants, she was hardly alone, but Ginger understood the sentiment. "What will you do now?"

"I'm out already. I've got a suite at Brown's Hotel, where I'll be going directly from here." Her face brightened. "I'm so looking forward to the change. It'll be a splendid living arrangement. The quality of the guests that come through will keep me entertained."

"And cause your hand to cramp," Ambrosia mumbled. "With all the writing."

Lady Whitmore's nose pointed upwards. "I only write what I see, and I'm often complimented for my efforts to keep everyone informed. One can't trust the journalist to tell the whole story anymore, can one?"

"Where does the Foote family come from?" Ginger asked. She was more than just a little curious about who her new neighbours might be.

"They're English but are returning to London after five years in Canada. Mr. Foote was a secretary to Lord Byng." She tutted. "Such a shame what happened."

"You're referring to the King-Byng affair?" Ginger stated.

Lady Whitmore's chin inched up. "Yes, of course."

The affair had dominated the headlines. Lord Byng, until recently, had been governor general in Canada. A recent scandal involving the prime minister of Canada, Mackenzie King, had caused Lord Byng to quit his position.

"I think the Canadian prime minister should've respected the governor general's decision, whatever that might have been," Lady Whitmore said with a tone that suggested she was personally affronted. "He represents the King."

Ambrosia sipped her tea, then returned the cup to its saucer. "For once, Lady Whitmore and I agree."

Ginger took the other side. "Canada is a sovereign nation, and perhaps it's time the Crown let the colonies make their own decisions, good or bad."

"Your American upbringing is showing, Ginger," Ambrosia said.

Lady Whitmore tutted. "I don't trust Americans. Not since the rebellion."

Ginger laughed. "You say that as if you were alive during the War of Independence."

"See," Ambrosia said with a note of accusation. "The British don't refer to that particular conflict as the War of Independence. It was a rebellion, through and through."

Lady Whitmore sighed again. "If only the Loyalists had won. Such a shame."

Ginger thought a change of subject was in order. "What other information do you have on the family? Besides Mr. Foote's former occupation."

"There's Mrs. Foote and their two daughters, Patricia and Charlotte," Lady Whitmore said. "I'm told they're nine years apart in age, so I imagine there's a story there somewhere. And Mrs. Foote's elderly father, a Mr. Rothwell, will be living with them as well."

Lady Whitmore picked up her teacup. "The eldest daughter is around Miss Gold's age, I'm told—or rather, Lady Davenport-Witt, now. Have you heard from the happy couple?"

"They've returned from their wedding journey in Greece this week," Ginger returned.

"I thought they were going to be abroad until Christmas."

Ginger blinked at the astute lady. "Yes, but Lord Davenport-Witt was required back in London, so they had to cut their trip short."

Lady Whitmore, her eyes glinting with the

prospect of juicy gossip, pushed on. "What could be so important that it would draw a new groom away from his bride?"

Ginger flicked a palm. She could only imagine it had something to do with Charles' continued involvement with the British secret service. But Felicia had quoted an urgent family and business matter, which was the excuse Ginger recited to her guest.

"But it's of no consequence," Ginger continued. "Felicia says she was quite ready to return to England, eager to begin her duties as the mistress of Witt House."

"Such a lovely residence," Lady Whitmore said reservedly, not quite reining in her disappointment at the less-than-exciting news. She set her teacup on the table, then smiled. "I do hope you ladies won't be offended if I take my leave. I simply have so much to do, and those removal men need constant supervision." She stood. As Ginger moved to get to her feet, Lady Whitmore lifted a palm. "Please don't bother yourself in your condition. I'm not leaving London. We'll have the opportunity to see each other again."

The same wind that had brought her in carried her out. Ginger laughed as she listened to Pippins rushing to get Lady Whitmore's shawl.

Ambrosia rolled her bulbous eyes, then finished her tea.

2

*G*inger was over the moon when Felicia arrived. Felicia's skin was bronzed pleasingly —as sunbathing had become fashionable when the indomitable Coco Chanel had accidentally got sunburned and returned from the Riviera with a suntan—from the Mediterranean sun. Felicia's dark hair was neatly shingled at her neckline, and her Clara Bow lips were thick with red lipstick. Her former sister-in-law smiled as her eyes landed on Ginger, and she hurried over to her.

"Ginger, darling, how I missed you!"

"And I you!" Ginger said with pure joy. "You look fabulous! Can I assume that married life is going well?"

"Very well," Felicia gushed. "Charles and I are soulmates, darling. I do love being Lady Davenport-Witt."

"It suits you, love," Ginger said, then held her stomach as it tightened again.

Felicia's eyes rounded. "Are you all right?"

"I'm fine," Ginger insisted. The pain subsided, and her muscles relaxed. "It appears the babe is eager to get started on things."

Felicia smiled. "I like her already. Brave, bold, ready to take on the world."

"We don't know if it's a girl."

"Then I like him already, but my intuition says it's a girl."

Ginger's intuition was saying the same thing, but time would tell. She stared at Felicia, who looked radiant and happy. A relief, since Ginger knew Felicia and Charles hadn't been due back from Greece for another few weeks.

"You're back early," she said. "Is everything all right?"

Felicia lowered herself into one of the armchairs that flanked the fireplace in the sitting room. "Charles got a telegram while we were in Greece. He's a consultant for the government, you know. I don't really understand what he does, and he insists I don't worry my 'pretty little head' over it."

It was clear by Felicia's tone she felt patronised. "Be glad he has something of import to do," Ginger said encouragingly. "Men need to feel like they're contributing to society somehow, that they have a reason to get up in the morning. It's especially difficult for those born to privilege."

"I suppose you're right," Felicia said as she peeled off her gloves. "Endless sunny days can become tedious. I'm eager to start decorating Witt House anyway, though I'd really like your help. I suppose you'll be off your feet for a while?"

"Until the baby is born and for some time after that."

"I can wait. I'd rather spend my time practising being an aunt!"

Ginger smiled. "You will be a fantastic aunt. In the meantime, shall I ring for tea?"

"If you don't mind my staying for a while," Felicia said. "And I have removed my gloves."

Ginger rang the bell, then looked back at Felicia, who was staring out the window.

"Has Lady Whitmore moved out?" Felicia asked.

"Yes. A new family by the name of Foote has moved in."

"I believe they've arrived." Felicia shifted the chair for a better view. "Shall I report what I see?" She glanced over her shoulder and grinned. "It's a way to pass the time."

"By all means," Ginger said, eager for the diversion. "I can't bear to get back onto my swollen feet to look for myself. Please, be my eyes and ears."

Felicia stood back from the window to not be spotted spying, a position Ginger found amusing. With a lift of her dainty chin, Felicia began her report.

"There's a middle-aged gentleman, Mr. Foote, I gather, long face, tight mouth with an overly large moustache, and a hat pulled down deeply over a long brow."

"Your eyesight is tremendous," Ginger said with a note of admiration.

Felicia glanced over her shoulder. "I've always been able to see well, especially when it comes to distance." She returned her attention to the activity outside. "A lady, I presume Mrs. Foote, with questionable taste in fashion and a matching sour expression, is speaking sternly to a younger girl, perhaps a little older than Scout. Oh, a young lady has stepped out of the motorcar—another daughter, I presume, but older perhaps—closer to my age and rather better dressed than her mother."

"What's she wearing?" Ginger asked, intrigued.

"An ombré coat with a striped fur collar that runs the length of the opening from hem to hem. The coat has three plaits on the back." Felicia's head turned, her attention drawn elsewhere. "Another motorcar has pulled up."

"More family?"

"A chauffeur has exited and, strangely, has passed by the passenger to the rear—oh, it appears that he is removing a wheelchair."

"A wounded soldier?" Ginger said. Now that the Great War was over there were plenty of soldiers convalescing.

Felicia's smile turned upside down. "Nothing as exciting as that. The chauffeur and Mr. Foote are assisting an elderly gentleman."

"That must be Mr. Rothwell," Ginger said. "He's Mrs. Foote's father. Lady Whitmore was here for tea and related the news about the family."

"The older gentleman is scowling at Mr. Foote. A family of crosspatches, I would say." Felicia chuckled. "It would appear that they are unhappy about moving into the old Whitmore place. What did Lady Whitmore have to say about them?"

"They've come from Canada."

"Canadians? I've always found them to be a cheery bunch."

"No, English. Mr. Foote was a secretary to Lord Byng, the former governor general there. Apparently, it didn't go well in the end with the current prime minister, and they've come back with their tails between their legs."

"I suppose that explains things."

Felicia's brows knitted together.

"What is it?" Ginger asked.

"It appears the younger girl is carrying a cat." Felicia turned to Ginger. "You do see it, don't you?"

"See what?"

"The Foote family is a reflection of your own. You and Basil, me and Scout, Grandmama, and Boss."

Ginger shifted in her chair, seeking a more comfortable position. "It's hardly a unique configuration. However, if Mrs. Foote is also large with child—"

Felicia wrinkled her nose. "Not that I can tell." She sighed and fell back into the chair. "They've gone inside. Nothing more to report, I'm afraid."

"I'm certain I'll have a chance to meet them in person in the near future," Ginger said. "Shall I ring for lunch? I'm beginning to feel peckish."

Ginger rang the bell for Lizzie, then turned back to Felicia. "You must tell me more about your time in Greece. I've never been there, you know, and I'm dreadfully envious."

"Greece is fabulous, if not a little, er . . ." Felicia couldn't keep a blush from spreading over her cheeks. ". . . hedonistic."

Ginger laughed. "The ancient Greeks didn't share our conservative nature, particularly those of us who align with the Church of England."

"Indeed! I must wonder at Charles taking me there

for our wedding journey. Or perhaps that's why. A swift education in the human anatomy."

"I'm certain he only had his mind on white beaches and blue sea. The epitome of romance."

Felicia's blush deepened. "I can assure you; there was no lacking in the romance department."

"How wonderful. It sounds like the perfect time away."

Felicia sighed contentedly. "It was. But now, alas, here we are. You off your feet and me with a husband gone who knows where."

"Husbands, as a matter of course, disappear who knows where. I have no idea where Basil is at the moment or if he even has a case he's working on. He's being stubbornly closed-lipped about his work these days."

"And quite right to be so, knowing you. Despite your condition, you would throw yourself into the next murder."

"I do love a good puzzle."

"Perhaps you should stick to the crossword or jigsaw variety for the time being."

"I've been doing plenty of those," Ginger said just as Lizzie arrived with a tray of tea and small sandwiches. "You may set the tray on the table by Lady Davenport-Witt," she instructed.

"Yes, madam." Lizzie carefully walked across the

Persian carpet, placed the tray in front of Felicia, and curtsied. "Good day, my lady."

Felicia smiled and offered Ginger a knowing look. Before today, Lizzie had always greeted Felicia as Miss Gold. When Ginger had arrived in London, she'd been addressed as "my lady", and now she was simply Mrs. Reed or "madam". How things had changed.

"Thank you, Lizzie," Ginger said. "How is everything downstairs?"

"Very good, madam. All the talk is about the new family moving in across the street. Did you know that one of the maids, Abby Green is her name, is a good friend of my mum's? Small world, as they say."

"How nice for both of you," Ginger said.

"It is, madam. Is there anything else you need?"

Ginger glanced at Felicia, who offered a slight shake of her head.

"Nothing at the moment, Lizzie."

"Just ring if you need anything else, madam." Lizzie bobbed at the knees, then left the room.

After a few nibbles and sips, Ginger asked, "So what do you plan on doing with the rest of your day?"

Felicia lifted her shoulders. "I don't know. Perhaps I should start a new book."

Felicia had found a modicum of success writing mystery novels under the name of Frank Gold.

"Charles thinks I should keep writing," she added,

"since I enjoy doing so. It's more of a hobby than a job in his eyes. At least, he says, until the children come. My editor is waiting for an outline, but I just don't have a good idea." She glanced out the window towards the house across Mallowan Court. "Unless . . ."

"Unless what?"

"I set a murder on a quiet London street in a large dark house with a gloomy family moving into it." Felicia's eyes brightened as inspiration hit. "And one of them is murdered!"

3

*T*he next day the house was abuzz with gossip about the new neighbours. Ginger and Basil, along with Scout and Ambrosia, enjoyed breakfast together in the morning room, a bright area with windows facing the patio in the back garden.

"Mrs. Schofield says that the elderly Mr. Crispin Rothwell was once a man about town and that she and Mr. Schofield shared acquaintances with him," Ambrosia said.

Ginger's mind conjured an image of her elderly, outspoken neighbour. "You say that as if you doubt her account."

Ambrosia shifted in her seat. "You know Mrs. Schofield. She's been known to stretch the truth. However, Mr. Rothwell did have a reputation in those days. Though I didn't frequent London in my younger years, I did read about him in the newspapers."

Ginger raised a brow in interest. "What kind of reputation?"

Ambrosia flicked her ring-covered fingers—she preferred the gems, her rubies, and sapphires—and though her fingers were crooked and the skin on her hands veiny and wrinkled, she never ceased adorning them with jewels.

"Oh, the usual," she said. "He made the rounds with the ladies, flaunted his riches, demanded attention at all the parties. It wasn't a surprise when he went broke. Now that news made all the headlines. 'Socialite Mogul Hits Bottom.'"

"I had no idea," Ginger said. "Did you, Basil?"

"Mr. Rothwell's heyday was a little before my time," Basil answered with a grin, "but I'm sure my parents would've heard something about him. Obviously, he married, presuming Mrs. Foote is his biological child."

"Oh, yes," Ambrosia continued, looking quite delighted to be the source of information for a change rather than the recipient. "He'd been engaged to a Miss Constance Mansfield. She, though not particularly beautiful, came from a very wealthy family. Gossip abounded as to when the marriage would occur, and if indeed it would—after such a long engagement and with the way Mr. Rothwell carried on with the ladies—but a date was set soon after he lost his fortune." Ambrosia paused to sip her tea, then added, "Talk was that Miss Mansfield married out of duty to her own father's wishes not to create a spectacle by breaking off the engagement. Honour and duty above all, I suppose."

"Lizzie is acquainted with one of Mrs. Foote's maids," Ginger said. "Abby Green, who is a friend of Lizzie's mother. Lizzie has insinuated that this Abby is unhappy in her position, even after such a short period of time."

Ambrosia stiffened. "The maids are sharing confidences?"

"Not at all," Ginger said. "But it's hard to hide one's lack of joy if one is unhappy with one's employer."

Ambrosia wasn't consoled. "If one is unhappy, one should find new employment."

"It's not always that easy," Ginger said. "One needs a good reference to move to a new position, and if you upset your current employer, well, you can see how it's a vicious cycle."

"I'm eager to make their acquaintance and get the initial introductions over with," Basil said. "It's not necessary to be the best of friends with one's neighbours, but one must be cordial."

"I like Miss Charlotte."

All eyes shot to Scout. So engaged were the adults in their discussions about the new family, they'd lost sight of the lad in their midst.

"When did you meet her?" Ginger asked.

Scout, though small for a boy of twelve, was clearly approaching puberty. His facial features were sharpening, his shoulders broadening, and occasionally, his voice cracked. He averted his gaze, but his discomfort at blurting out his news was evident in the rosy hue overtaking his cheeks.

"Just outside, when I took Boss for a walk."

Ginger glanced at Basil, who hid his grin behind a napkin, ostensibly patting sausage grease from his mouth. Scout played with Boss outside regularly, but always in the back garden where there was space to run and near the small stable where the horses were housed. The front garden wasn't nearly as spacious, and a wrought-iron fence ran along the edge of the property and the road.

"Oh?" Ginger said.

"I was curious about the new people. Miss Charlotte was in their front garden with her cat."

"You spoke to her?" Basil asked.

Scout jerked, his eyes growing round. "No, not at all. I don't think she even saw me. I heard the mother call her. That's how I know her name." He buried his chin in his chest as if he suffered a deep regret over speaking out. He muttered, "She seemed nice."

Ginger patted Scout on the back, feeling pity for his discomfiture. "I'm certain she is, as I am that the whole family will prove to be. Moving is a difficult exercise, and they've come all the way from Canada."

Pippins entered, holding a silver tray in one hand. "A message came for you, madam."

"Oh? From whom I wonder," Ginger replied.

Pippins' blue eyes glistened with apparent knowledge but he stayed quiet as Ginger picked up the card. "Mrs. Foote is asking me for tea this afternoon."

"You mustn't," Ambrosia said with a tsk. "Not in your condition."

Ginger held in her grimace. Why must the most natural things like motherhood be hidden and disguised as if they were something to be ashamed about? However, some social requirements could not be changed, not in a moment, anyway.

"Very well. Pippins, please offer my regrets, but extend an invitation for Mrs. Foote to join me here at Hartigan House for the same time."

"Yes, madam," Pippins said before bowing and leaving the morning room.

Turning to Ambrosia, Ginger asked, "Would you like to join us?"

"I've had quite enough of having tea with the

neighbours for this week, thank you," Ambrosia said. "I've taken to having a lie-down in the afternoons, and I don't think today will be an exception."

"Very well," Ginger said. "Perhaps I'll ring Felicia. She's very curious about the Foote family and is no doubt looking for something to do."

WHEN FELICIA HAD FIRST BEEN GIVEN the tour of Charles' house on Wilton Crescent in Belgravia, she couldn't believe her good fortune that she would one day be the mistress of such a fine residence. Witt House made Hartigan House look modest in size, though Ginger, with Felicia's help, had done wonders in modernising the decor.

Witt House, in comparison, was dreadfully out of touch with the times, thoroughly locked in the Edwardian age, and with so many rooms in need of a change, Felicia hardly knew where to start.

"The bedroom," she told Charles as they shared breakfast in the morning room.

"I'm sorry, love," Charles said with a grin. "It would be my pleasure, but you know I'm needed in the House of Lords."

Felicia smacked him playfully on the arm. "I meant as a place to begin decorating."

"Ah. I missed the introduction to the subject change."

"I'm afraid I've been known to think aloud on occasion. And so, staying on subject, I think I'll start decorating the bedroom. Or . . ." She tilted her head to the door behind them. "Should I start in the sitting room?"

"Start wherever you like, Lady Davenport-Witt," Charles said affectionately. "This house is your canvas."

"If only I were an artist. Ginger is so much better at this kind of thing than I am."

Felicia's lower lip moved out, and she was aware of her pout. Really, a dreadful habit for a lady. She pulled it back in. "I just wish she wasn't so housebound. She's brilliant with fashion and design and loves it so. I just couldn't bear her disappointment if I choose the wrong thing."

"If you don't like something once it's done, you can simply change it," Charles said. "You're overthinking the matter."

"Perhaps you're right," Felicia conceded.

"Why not ask a friend for help. One of your bridesmaids?"

"Doris might be able to help, but . . ."

"But what?"

"My friends are all an awful lot like me." Pampered, entitled, and not used to having a single original thought. Felicia grimaced to herself at her harsh judgement and marvelled at how quickly she had moved from being a bright young thing, without an apparent care in the world, to being an earl's wife and overwhelmed by the prospect of managing such a prominent residence. She even found it difficult keeping track of the staff, and now the cook wanted her to approve the menu each day. As if she knew a speck about cooking!

And now that Felicia was married, her friends seemed to have forgotten about her, too busy searching for the next carefree—and often careless—experience. It was like Felicia had gone through a door, entering one world and leaving another parallel version behind.

Felicia continued, "They're very skilled at doing nothing much at all."

Charles reached for Felicia's hands and gripped them. "You are a very talented lady, Felicia, even if you've yet to settle into your place. I know this life change is a lot for you to take on all at once. Take your time to get used to things here. Nothing is so urgent that you have to make sweeping changes overnight."

"That's true," Felicia said, feeling a little better. "I could visit Ginger again. She must find being confined to her house terribly boring. I can make it my task to divert her!"

"That's my girl," Charles said. He kissed her nose

then stood to leave. "I'm afraid I'll be back late again tonight. Needs must. Don't wait up."

Felicia's cheer dissipated as she watched her husband exit, and with him, it felt to her, all the light in the room.

Leaving the last bit of her toast on her plate, Felicia pushed away from the table. The house about her felt oppressive, and she had a sudden urge to get out of it. How ironic that she'd spent the last year desiring to get away from her grandmother and a house full of people, only to be missing it so now.

In the distance, Felicia heard the ringing of the telephone. There were three in the house—and if that wasn't a symbol of their affluence, Felicia didn't know what was—one in the hall upstairs, one in Charles' study, and one in the drawing room.

Shortly, a young maid, Daphne, came with a message.

"Mrs. Reed rang for you, my lady," Daphne said. "She's invited you for tea this afternoon to meet her new neighbour."

*a*s it turned out, Ginger's guest arrived before Felicia did. Alerted by the long chimes of the doorbell, Ginger headed for the drawing room, instructing Pippins as she went. "Take a bit of time to gather her coat, Pips, so that I can get settled. Then tell Grace we'll be ready for tea in ten minutes."

"Yes, madam."

Ginger disappeared behind the tall doors of the drawing room just as Pippins opened the entrance door. She could hear his low baritone voice. "Please do come in. Allow me to take your coats."

Coats? Mrs. Foote hadn't come alone. Who was the mystery guest?

The drawing room was even more spacious than the sitting room and had the distinction of being graced with a shiny black grand piano. Ginger mused that she hadn't played in some time and made a mental note to use some of the extra time spent at home to exercise her fingers as well. The walls were papered in ivory and black geometric shapes, contrasting with the rose sheers that framed the tall windows. She settled into one of the green-velvet chairs, then pushed herself into a standing position when Pippins entered.

"Mrs. Foote and Miss Patricia Foote to see you, madam."

The resemblance between the two ladies was minimal, with the elder looking fatigued and having a tendency to slump, while her daughter stood tall with a haughty expression on her youthful face.

Ginger smiled as she extended a hand. "Welcome Mrs. Foote, Miss Foote. So kind of you to consider my request to convene here."

Neither Foote lady reciprocated with a smile. Mrs. Foote's eyes scanned Ginger's dress, her gaze pausing on Ginger's rounded girth.

"Once we were informed of your delicate condition, we were happy to. We won't stay long."

Before Ginger could ask them to take a seat, Mrs. Foote held out a glass bottle which appeared to be filled with a thick, dark-brown substance.

"It's maple syrup," Mrs. Foote explained. "A gift from our time in Canada."

Ginger was moved. "How very kind and unexpected. We had this often in Boston. It's exquisite."

Mrs. Foote looked thoroughly disappointed. "Most British people haven't had the pleasure."

"I've missed it so!" Ginger said, hoping to appease. "I can't wait to try it again. Pippins, please take this lovely gift to the kitchen."

Pippins accepted the bottle of syrup, bowed slightly, then left the three ladies alone.

Ginger motioned to the mint-green settee. "Please have a seat."

Mrs. Foote and Miss Foote took either end of the settee, both staring ahead as if they were eager to get the obligatory visits to the neighbours out of the way.

"I've rung for tea," Ginger said.

Mrs. Foote replied, "That would be lovely."

"Did you like it in Canada?"

"Very much so," Mrs. Foote said. "Though it did get terribly cold in the winters."

Miss Foote sniffed, and Ginger addressed her, smiling in an attempt to make the younger lady more relaxed. "Are you happy to be back in London?"

"Oh yes. Canada is nice, but rather barbaric. There is *nothing* to do."

"Not even in Toronto?" Ginger asked.

After another sniff, Miss Foote replied, "We lived

in Ottawa. Parliament Hill is still under construction after that nasty fire. And there was far too much snow."

Grace, one of the housemaids, arrived with a tea tray and placed it on the low table between them.

"Thank you, Grace."

Grace curtsied. "Madam. Can I bring you anything else?"

"That will be all for now," Ginger said. She didn't want to prolong this meeting any longer than necessary. How she was envying Ambrosia, wishing for a lie-down herself.

Ginger poured three cups of tea, leaving the fourth empty.

Mrs. Foote noticed. "Were you expecting someone else?"

"I invited my sister-in-law to join us," Ginger said as she handed out the floral-patterned teacups on their matching saucers, "but she must be stuck in traffic."

CHARLES HAD GIVEN Felicia one of his motorcars to drive—a classy new, shiny black Vauxhall with a polished chrome bonnet, a flat roof that folded back, transforming the machine into an open-top in the warmer summer months, spoked tyres with wide, shiny black mudguards, and large "bug-eye" headlamps. Felicia prided herself on being a better driver than

Ginger, though she wouldn't dare say it to Ginger's face.

It didn't take long to get from Belgravia to Kensington, especially in the afternoon when the traffic was lighter. Felicia motored into Mallowan Court, slowing as she approached Hartigan House, and her heart squeezed a little with fondness. She chided herself. The place hadn't even been her home for long, only three years, yet like a child, she was feeling an undefinable melancholy.

She parked and stepped out, and that was when she spotted the man across the street huddled over in a wheelchair. Wearing a wool coat, hat, and scarf, the man also had a small rug on his lap for warmth.

The way he narrowed his deep-set eyes at her, his gaze moving up and down as if he were a much younger man admiring a young lady, unnerved her. She threw her shoulders back in defiance and raised a hand. "Good day, sir. Welcome to the neighbourhood."

The man frowned and collapsed in on himself even more, if it were possible. He barked at a man who waited near the entrance of the house, who ran to his employer, took charge of the wheelchair, and steered the elderly man inside.

Felicia snorted and mumbled to herself, "What a sad old gentleman."

Pippins, who always surprised Felicia with his

unexpected nimbleness and apparent sixth sense, greeted her at the door.

"Good day, my lady," he said with new deference, and Felicia found she missed the way he used to call her "miss" with a cheery glint in his eye.

"Hello, Pippins. Mrs. Reed is expecting me."

Pippins took her coat and scarf. "Indeed, she is. She awaits you in the drawing room. Mrs. Foote and Miss Patricia Foote are with her."

Felicia braced herself as she entered. If the Foote ladies were even a little as irascible as their family patriarch, then she was in for a trying time.

Felicia knew her way to the drawing room, an immediate right from the front doors through the entrance hall. She tapped on the tall double door before letting herself in.

"Hello! I do apologise for my tardiness."

"Not at all," Ginger said with a notable look of relief, which Felicia thought to be inauspicious. "I'll ring for a fresh pot of tea."

Felicia settled into the empty chair. It'd been a while since she'd been in the grand room—the first time since moving out to get married. Her mind flashed back to when she and Grandmama had first moved into Hartigan House and how she and Ginger had transformed the room into the modern, airy space it was now. She tried to imagine a similar alteration of the sitting room at Witt House, but her mind refused to cooperate for some reason. It reminded her of those times when she'd suffered from the inability to write, paralysed by the first blank page. She had the skills, but the flow of creativity was inexplicably quenched.

"Felicia?"

Ginger's voice brought Felicia back to the present, and she focused on the guests who were eyeing her with quiet curiosity.

Ginger jumped into the introductions. "Felicia, this is Mrs. Foote and Miss Foote, our new neighbours who have taken Whitmore House. Mrs. Foote and Miss Foote, allow me to introduce Lady Davenport-Witt."

Miss Foote's eyes rounded into large saucers, and her small mouth fell open. "You're Lady Davenport-Witt? Recently married to Lord Davenport-Witt?"

Even though the young lady's shock and exuberance were a little embarrassing, Felicia couldn't help but feel pleased with the obvious envy and admiration.

Felicia held out a gloved hand. "I am."

"I thought you said you'd invited your sister-in-law, Mrs. Reed," Mrs. Foote said coolly. "Not that meeting Lady Davenport-Witt isn't a pleasant surprise."

"Though not technically sisters-in-law now," Ginger said, "Lady Davenport-Witt is the sister of my late husband, Lord Daniel Gold. In my heart, we will always be sisters."

Felicia wanted to hug Ginger, and if it weren't for the prying gazes of the Foote ladies, she just might've. As it was, she had to fight back the tears that burned in the back of her eyes. Grandmama and Ginger were the only family she had, and now that she'd moved away and started her own life with Charles, the preciousness of those relationships had only grown dearer. She settled for reaching over the gap between their chairs and squeezing Ginger's arm.

The Foote ladies stared at the show of affection as if they were watching two primates behaving like animals in a zoo.

Grace arrived with a new pot of tea, curtsying before setting it on the table and taking the cooled pot away.

Ginger poured for her, and after a sip, Felicia said, "I understand you've recently returned from Canada?"

"Yes. The journey over was treacherous."

"Mummy spent most of the time casting up her accounts for the fish."

Mrs. Foote gasped at her daughter. "Patricia!"

Miss Foote smirked. "It's true. We were all a bit sick at first, but Mummy never got her sea legs."

"I prefer solid ground," her mother returned. "Thank you very much."

"I like London," Patricia said, staring at Felicia. "More for people our age to do. Can you recommend any clubs, Lady Davenport-Witt, or has marriage clipped your wings?"

Felicia blinked at Miss Foote's audacity.

Ginger jumped in. "More tea, Miss Foote?"

"No, thank you," she said. She patted her slender figure. "I'm about to float away as it is."

"You have a younger daughter, Mrs. Foote," Ginger said. "Apparently, she and my son Samuel—we call him Scout—have already met."

Mrs. Foote narrowed her eyes, barely concealing her displeasure. "How old is your son?"

"He's twelve."

Mrs. Foote relaxed moderately at Ginger's answer, and Felicia perceived that she was a rather protective mother. "Charlotte is thirteen. Very bright for a girl. I'm not sure what to do with her."

"She could go to university," Ginger said lightly. "I have a degree from Boston University."

"In America?" Miss Foote said, once again with eyes glinting with both admiration and envy.

"Yes," Ginger said. "It's a shame for a mind to be wasted, simply because it's housed in the body of a female, isn't that right, Felicia?"

Felicia nodded. "If a lady desires to go, that is." She had never felt the need, but she wondered now that her opportunity had passed if she'd one day regret it.

"I'm afraid my father has old-fashioned ideas," Mrs. Foote said, "shared by my husband."

Miss Foote's expression had turned cold, and Felicia got the distinct impression she didn't care for either man in her family.

The conversation continued in a stiff and downcast manner, and Felicia was about to suggest she put a record on the gramophone when Ginger winced and shifted in her chair, draping an arm around her extended stomach.

"Is everything all right?" Felicia asked.

Ginger's smile was pinched. "Oh, yes. Just a bit uncomfortable."

Mrs. Foote shot her daughter a look then stood. "We should go and let you rest, Mrs. Reed."

"I'm happy we had a chance to meet before . . ." Ginger pointed to her midsection, "I get dreadfully busy."

Felicia stopped Ginger before she tried to get to her feet. "I'll walk them to the door."

In his omnipresent way, Pippins appeared with the coats and scarves belonging to Mrs. and Miss Foote.

Polite salutations were extended, and Felicia couldn't stop a breath of relief from escaping when the two dour ladies disappeared behind the door. She returned to Ginger, congratulating her.

"What a wonderful ruse! I didn't think I could take another second of their dreary pessimism."

Ginger winced. "I fear I wasn't playacting. I really am suffering discomfort. Be a dear and help me up the stairs. I'm in need of a lie-down."

Felicia rushed to Ginger's side, her heart pinching with worry, and did as she was bidden.

he next morning, Ginger awoke to sharp belly pains and emitted an involuntary cry.

Basil shot up in the four-poster bed they shared. "Love?"

Ginger winced as the pain slowly subsided. "It's just another one of those annoying Braxton Hicks events. I'll be fine."

Basil, obviously unconvinced, got out of bed and reached for his dressing gown. "I'm ringing Dr. Longden."

"No need—" Ginger was about to tell Basil not to bother the doctor but was stopped by another pain as her stomach tightened.

Basil scowled, then raced across the plush green-and-white Persian carpet and out of the bedroom.

Once again, Ginger mentally counted the months since her last womanly episode and wrinkled her nose when she came to less than nine. From her perspective, her stomach was a mountain under the white sheets, and she patted the mound. "I know we both want to get this over with, but let's hang on for a little while longer, shall we?"

A tap on the door produced Lizzie, Ginger's rather frazzled-looking young maid, with a tea tray in hand. "Forgive my intrusion, Mrs. Reed, but Mr. Reed instructed me to bring you a cup of tea."

"Thank you, Lizzie. I'm glad you're here. I fear I'll need to use the bathroom before I indulge."

Lizzie, a petite girl with a pixie-like face, was well versed in helping Ginger get about in these last weeks of her tender state. She wrapped an arm around Ginger's girth and helped her to her feet. Ginger paused to ensure there wasn't any dampness—she'd delivered a couple of babies in her life and knew the breaking of the amniotic fluid was a sure sign that labour had to occur. Thankfully, it was only her bladder that threatened to fail her. At least the bathroom wasn't too far down the corridor.

By the time she'd finished her business, Basil was in the corridor waiting. His eyes scanned her long white-cotton gown; the lace hem lifted higher in the front from the baby weighing heavily inside. He rushed to her side, taking her arm.

"I'm quite all right," Ginger insisted. She wasn't infirm, after all. And not so front-heavy that she would fall over.

Basil insisted she take his arm, and she complied. Leaning into her husband for any purpose was something she enjoyed. As if she were fragile and in hospital, he tucked her back into bed. She almost berated him for it except that another strong contraction came.

Basil's hazel eyes, wrinkling more deeply at the corners, stared at her hard with concern. "Are you—"

"I don't think so," Ginger said, but she wasn't sure. Not entirely. It wasn't like she'd ever done this before.

"Dr. Longden will be here shortly," Basil said.

Lizzie, who'd stepped to the side while the couple settled into their place, said, "Would you like your tea now, Mrs. Reed? I've brought two cups."

"That would be splendid," Basil said, replying for the two of them. "Extra sugar for Mrs. Reed."

Lizzie poured the tea, added the sugar, then brought the tray to the bedside table. Basil thanked her, and she curtsied. "Is there anything else, sir?"

"That will be all for now," Basil replied. "We'll ring the bell if we need you again."

"Yes, sir, madam," Lizzie said with another curtsey, then left them alone.

Basil, sitting next to Ginger as she was propped up in bed, closed his eyes and let out a long breath. Ginger reached for his hand. As new and nerve-racking as this experience was for her, she realised that Basil was also bearing the weight of the uncertainty of their future and the adventure of bringing a new life into the world.

"It's going to be fine," she said.

"I know," he answered. His eyes flickered open, and he sipped his tea.

Tapping on the door was followed by Pippins' voice. Without stepping into the room, he pronounced, "Dr. Longden is here."

Basil took Ginger's teacup and placed it with his own on the tray before shifting off the bed and onto his feet. With long strides, he met the doctor and shook his hand.

"Thank you for coming at short notice and so quickly."

"Of course, Chief Inspector Reed." Dr. Longden was at the back end of middle-age, with greying hair and thick round spectacles, new Ginger thought, that appeared to be rather heavy for his nose. "It's part of my duties to be ready at all times," he said, his gaze moving to the windows and the house across the court. "Day or night, especially when a baby is preparing to enter the world." He placed his black medical bag at the end of the bed and approached Ginger.

"Mrs. Reed. I understand you're having some discomfort?"

"Just those annoying pretend labour contractions. I fear we may have called on you prematurely."

"Nonsense. It's always better to be safe than sorry, I always say." He turned to Basil. "If you could give us a few moments' privacy, I'd like to make a quick examination."

"Certainly." Basil nearly skipped out of the room to escape what was to come, and Ginger bit her lip to keep from laughing out loud.

"Poor man," she said once Basil had left the room. "This has all been a bit much for him, I'm afraid."

"Giving birth isn't for the faint of heart," was the doctor's response. Then at Ginger's glimmer of alarm, modified his sentiment. "Mothers are the bravest of us all. It's why God gave the privilege of procreation to them." He smiled. "You'll do fine, I'm sure. Now, let's have a look."

GINGER RELUCTANTLY AGREED to remain bedridden for a week to prevent early labour. With her doctor and her husband staring sternly at her from the foot of the bed, she could hardly protest. What was a week in the scheme of things, really, if it meant a safe entry into the world for her little one?

Basil had brought her several books from their small library to appease her, though it was the newly released Agatha Christie novel, *The Murder of Roger Ackroyd*, that interested her the most. She read as she ate a breakfast of eggs and toast and sugar-sweetened tea brought to her by Lizzie and was very intrigued by the clever character Monsieur Poirot.

However, one could only read so much before one needed to rest, and Ginger liked to mull the clues over, enjoy the process of deduction without rushing to the end to discover the conclusion.

Lizzie came for the tray, and at that moment, Ginger couldn't think of anything else she needed, but later she wished she had had her maid bring in a gramophone and play a record. She could ring the bell, but Ginger didn't want to act the part of the demanding invalid, requiring her staff to jump every minute at her beck and call. No, she'd wait a few minutes, perhaps close her eyes. She could always sing the tune to herself. She did rather like singing.

Oh blast! Only a few hours had passed, and she was bored to tears! The next six and a half days would be frightfully long.

Ginger was about to ring the bell despite her previous determination not to, when the most marvellous surprise happened—Felicia breezed into the room.

"Ginger, darling!" she said. "Pippins told me that

you've been put on bed rest. For a whole week? Is it true?"

"Unfortunately, yes," Ginger said, allowing herself a modicum of self-pity. "But seeing you has cheered me immensely."

Felicia deposited her handbag on a chair and removed her gloves one finger at a time. "You mustn't worry, dear. I'll visit every day to keep you company."

Ginger considered Felicia with a tilt of her head. "That's awfully kind of you, and though I do love your company, I'm really not in need of charity. What about your plans to redecorate Witt House?"

Felicia settled into the gold-and-white-striped armchair opposite the one occupied by her handbag and gloves and wiggled her manicured nails. "Witt House has been in its current state for many years. A few more weeks won't matter." Her eyes fell to the copy of *The Murder of Roger Ackroyd* sitting on Ginger's bedside table. "Don't tell me you've only begun reading that now? It's been out since June!"

"I'm ashamed to admit it," Ginger said, "but providence has reserved the pleasure, for now, a time when I truly need it."

"It's rather brilliant," Felicia said with a blush of literary excitement. "I'm not sure I can ever write another word, if that's the bar that's been raised."

"You're a fabulous mystery writer, Felicia."

"Yes, well, Mrs. Christie's editor didn't make her take a man's name, did he? I'll forever be known as Frank Gold."

"Must you, though?" Ginger asked. "Your last book did well. Surely there is room for negotiation. Perhaps a new series with your new name."

Felicia scoffed. "Lady Davenport-Witt? In retrospect, I think I'll stay with Frank Gold. Then, if people hate him, Lady Davenport-Witt's reputation will be saved."

Something outside caught Felicia's attention. "Are you expecting a doctor's visit?"

Ginger shook her head. "He was here just this morning. Why?"

"Because Dr. Longden has just driven up." Felicia pulled the curtains and took a closer look. "Yes, that's him. Though, he's headed to the Whitmore residence."

"The Foote residence now," Ginger corrected.

"Yes, quite right. Mrs. Foote is greeting him at the door, and she looks even grimmer than she did yesterday for tea, if that were possible."

Ginger had a sinking feeling. "Dr. Longden must be their family doctor as well. I do hope everything is all right."

Felicia continued her reporting. "Mr. Foote and his

pet moustache have stepped out. And now Miss Patricia Foote has stepped out. It appears she's in need of a cigarette. She's staring down the road, her foot tapping."

"Waiting for someone," Ginger said.

"Perhaps. Now the younger Miss Foote has joined them. They are having words. The younger Miss Foote looks like she's about to burst into tears, but, oh, she's distracted by a motorcar."

Ginger laughed. "Oh, Felicia, you're such a brick!"

Felicia laughed too. "If it helps you pass the time, I'm game." She turned back to the window. "It's a green two-seater with a soft white roof. An older model with a short, barrel-like bonnet. The kind with one tyre in the back."

"A Darmont-Morgan?" Ginger asked.

"Perhaps. A rather handsome man has stepped out, and Miss Foote is running towards him. Oh, Mr. Foote looks very unhappy at seeing this, and what? He's shaking a fist! Drat, it's November, and the window is closed. If I open it, they'll notice I'm watching, but I can't hear what they're saying."

"Such drama," Ginger said with a grin.

"Oh dear, Mr. Foote and the gentleman are nose to nose. I can almost see them spitting from here. Miss Foote is tugging on the gentleman's arm, pulling him away from her father."

Starting to envy Felicia's view out the window, Ginger sat upright. "Is this really happening, or are you using your storytelling gifts to amuse me?"

Felicia shot Ginger a serious look. "It's actually happening."

"I want to see." Ginger started to swing her legs over the side of the bed, but Felicia jumped to her feet, stopping her.

"No, Ginger. The doctor said to stay in bed."

"I'm permitted to use the bathroom."

Felicia cocked her head. "Then I'll assist you to the corridor." She glanced over her shoulder. "Besides, the show is over. Miss Foote has driven off with the young man, and Mr. Foote has stormed back inside. Only the young girl remains, and . . ."

"And?" Ginger pressed.

"What an odd little girl. She's smiling."

"It does seem a strange thing to find joy in," Ginger admitted.

"Oh, wait, Dr. Longden is emerging. He's frowning. Oh dear."

"What? Felicia?"

"An ambulance has just driven up. Dr. Longden doesn't look happy. He's stepped up to the driver now, is shaking his head, and has now waved them away."

"That means his patient wasn't saved," Ginger said gravely. "There's been a death."

"Just like in *The Murder of Roger Ackroyd*," Felicia said with wonder. "The doctor is summoned—"

"Stop!" Ginger said. "You mustn't give it away!"

6

*T*he news of Mr. Crispin Rothwell's death was in the papers by that same evening. Having pulled up one of the gold-and-white-striped chairs to Ginger's bedside, Basil sat with his legs crossed, two hands gripping the pages, and read the report.

"Mr. Crispin Rothwell of Mallowan Court, a long-time Londoner, known for his charisma and flamboyance, was declared deceased this afternoon, his end brought on by natural causes. Mr. Rothwell lived with his daughter, son-in-law, and two granddaughters. The family had only recently returned after spending several years in Canada. He was seventy-nine years of age."

He glanced up and mused, "I wonder who found the deceased?"

"It was the young girl, Charlotte Foote."

Basil raised a brow. "How do you know that?"

Ginger shrugged a shoulder. "Lizzie told me, having heard it from her mother's friend who works there." Ginger's mind went to the unusual family gathering Felicia had described. "Poor child."

"Indeed," Basil said. His eyes focused, once again, on the newspaper. "The family is planning a funeral service to take place at St. Stephen's, Gloucester Road, with details to follow."

Ginger worked her lips. "Natural causes?"

Basil snapped the paper closed, folded it, and set it on the bedside table. "Dr. Longden says he appears to have had a heart attack. He'd got pneumonia while in Canada, which weakened him."

"A shame," Ginger said. "I've only met the daughter and one granddaughter, and neither seemed the happy sort. How sad to add grief to their lot."

"It's the nature of things. Some die, and . . ." he nodded at Ginger's stomach, "some are born. Grief and joy, joy and grief."

Ginger smiled. "You're awfully philosophical today."

"Am I?" Basil ran a hand through his hair. "I think it's all the new grey that's suddenly appearing. I wonder, am I too old to be becoming a new parent?"

Ginger took Basil's hand and squeezed. Though

ten years her senior, Ginger found him incredibly handsome. Yes, his hazel eyes were framed with wrinkles and the grey in his temples was gradually becoming more prominent, but none of that ever took away from Ginger's affection. "You hardly have a choice, love. Besides, I'm not exactly a spring chicken."

Ginger carried a concern, having conceived for the first time in her thirties, and not for lack of trying. It had happened the same way for her mother; only her mother hadn't survived beyond the birth.

Ginger couldn't be blamed for worrying just a little, could she?

As if reading her mind, Basil kissed her hand. "Everything is going to be just fine. We'll be old but jolly parents to this baby, who will be loved and spoiled beyond compare."

"Not spoiled," Ginger said. "But most certainly loved."

BASIL INSISTED that Ginger indulge in a long nap, a request she was happy to oblige, and she gently woke to Lizzie bringing in a tray of tea and sandwiches.

"Oh, I didn't mean to disturb you, madam," she whispered.

"It's fine," Ginger returned. "I'm awake."

Lizzie, despite Ginger clearly being roused from

her sleep, tiptoed through the room, setting the tray on the table by the window. "Mrs. Beasley thought you'd like to awaken to a pot of tea."

"She's quite right. I'm rather famished. Do thank her."

"I will, madam. Now, Mr. Reed says you mustn't leave your bed. I'll prepare your tea and bring it to you."

"Mr. Reed is fussing needlessly," Ginger said. "But he can't keep me from going to the loo."

Ginger waddled—yes, she was feeling quite a lot like a duck these days—to the bathroom at the end of the corridor, and by the time she returned, Lizzie had her tea ready.

"Once you're settled, madam," Lizzie said, "I'll bring the tray over."

As Ginger hoisted herself onto the bed and under the covers, working to smooth the sheets out underneath herself and around her girth, Lizzie said, "Sad news about our new neighbours. They've only just moved and already have a death to contend with."

Ginger patted the bed beside her, indicating that she was ready for her tea. "Indeed. But Mr. Rothwell was aged. I suppose it was bound to happen."

Lizzie approached the bed and carefully placed the tray beside Ginger. "I suppose so," she said, "but Abby

—she's a friend of the family—well, I suppose I shouldn't gossip."

Ginger sipped her tea and then nibbled on a triangle of cucumber and salmon sandwich. "I could use a bit of entertaining, Lizzie. Go on."

"Well, madam, my ma says, Abby doesn't think Mr. Rothwell died of natural causes."

Ginger stilled and stared at her maid. "Are you saying Abby thinks he was murdered?"

"It sounds awful when you say it aloud, madam, and I'm sure she's wrong."

"Did she tell you why she thinks this? Is she the kind to see the dark side of things?"

"No, not at all. Abby's the cheery type."

"I see," Ginger said. She repeated her first question. "Why does Abby suspect foul play?"

"Well, that's it, madam. It's just a suspicion. She was working on the upper floor, near Mr. Rothwell's bedroom, and every member of the family had gone in and left again, one at a time, and each—according to Abby—was none too happy about the visit." Lizzie frowned. "I'm sure she's making something out of nothing."

"A family upset could've brought on a heart attack," Ginger said. "If Mr. Rothwell was disturbed enough."

"That's probably it, madam. Is there anything else you would like me to get for you?"

"That's all for now," Ginger said.

"Just ring the bell if you change your mind." Lizzie curtsied and left Ginger to her tea.

Picking up her Agatha Christie novel, Ginger endeavoured to focus on the crafted mystery, but her mind kept reverting to the enigmatic Foote family.

Had Mr. Rothwell's death been due to natural causes, or not?

7

*G*inger was entertained the next morning by another visit from Felicia.

"I had a premonition!" Felicia strutted into the bedroom wearing a navy-blue long-sleeve frock that had a gorgeous lace V-neck collar with a long bow tied at its base, and a faux-gemstone belt-buckle on the hip band. "Didn't I say my next book should be about this very thing?"

Ginger's fingers rubbed at Boss' neck as she regarded Felicia with a raised brow. "A situation where an elderly man succumbs to something as natural as death is hardly a prediction to be applauded."

Felicia waved away Ginger's sensible comment and stared out the window to the house with a black-crepe ribbon on the knocker. "I saw Mr. Rothwell two days ago."

"You did?"

"Yes, didn't I mention it? I parked out the front when I came here to visit, and Mr. Rothwell was sitting in his wheelchair, in quite a mood, refusing to return my greeting. He snapped at his assistant, who hurried to wheel him back inside. I don't know what caused Mr. Rothwell's need for a chair, but I don't picture him as the type to die in his sleep. He appeared to be far too stubborn for that."

Ginger wanted to laugh. "Even stubborn men can't stave off the angel of death when it comes."

Felicia flopped in her chair. "Oh, do let me have my fun, Ginger."

Ginger shifted uncomfortably in her bed, giving her pillows a fluffing. Boss looked at her with disapproval before curling into a ball beside her and closing his round brown eyes. "Don't tell me married life is boring you already."

"I'm not bored with Charles. But he works rather a lot, something I admit I never considered before. He always seemed to be available to me when I wanted him. It's this new position he's taken on. He apologises for the time but insists that it's a duty he can't forsake."

Ginger wonder if Charles' recent position with Stanley Baldwin's government was simply a desire to fulfil his duty, or if it was a cover for something more. Only Ginger knew of his past involvement with the

British secret service, particularly during the Great War, but surely not everything Charles did was tied to that.

Ginger's mind was brought back to Felicia, who was still speaking. "I hope you're not tiring of me, Ginger. I have been coming round a lot." She shimmied in her seat. "More than when I lived here."

"Felicia, love, you will always be welcome here. Witt House may be your new residence, but you must always consider Hartigan House your second home."

"Oh, thank you, Ginger. You don't know how much that means to me."

"Of course. Now, you must tell me if anything interesting is happening outside."

"Well . . ." Felicia twisted to stare out the window. "Actually, there is some activity. Mrs. Foote, dressed in black, has her younger daughter in tow, and now they're getting into the back seat of their motorcar. Their chauffeur is driving. Yes, there they go."

Ginger snorted. How had a play-by-play of someone in her neighbourhood simply leaving their house become her greatest source of entertainment?

"Oh," Felicia started. "Miss Foote has come outside, dressed in a coat and hat, but no gloves."

"In a hurry, then?" Ginger offered.

"She's looking at her wristwatch and scowling. Oh, she's turned on her heel and stormed back inside."

"Either her taxicab is late, or the young man has stood her up."

Felicia laughed. "See, it's not only me who finds the Foote behaviour amusing."

Ginger was beginning to think their behaviour was going beyond amusing to somewhat suspicious. Lizzie's words about Abby's concerns came to mind. "I wonder..."

Felicia spun to face Ginger. "What are you thinking, Ginger? Are you changing your mind about the innocence of Mr. Rothwell's death?"

"I've never claimed to believe innocence. Lizzie mentioned something of interest. Her friend Abby works as a maid for the Foote family. She inadvertently witnessed a hostile event." Ginger relayed the second-hand story about all the Foote family members visiting Mr. Rothwell in the hour before he died. "None of them was too happy after their encounter with the family patriarch."

Felicia sprang to her feet. "Shall I investigate for you? Not only can I be your eyes and ears, but I could also be your hands and feet and your mouthpiece."

"I don't know—"

"Are you saying that, if you weren't bound to your bed, you'd leave this alone and not enquire at least a little?"

"Well—"

"Then let me do it for you. Worst case, I get more inspiration for my next novel. Best case, we solve a murder!"

Ginger laughed, rousing Boss, who stretched out a hind leg. "Oh, Felicia. I do admire your enthusiasm. I suppose it wouldn't hurt to ask a few questions, discreetly, of course."

Felicia smiled brightly. "Of course. Now, where should I start?"

A RIBBON of excitement wound about Felicia's chest. She'd worked with Ginger as an assistant at Lady Gold Investigations, but her primary task was to open the mail and make the tea. On rare occasions, Ginger had asked her to take on minor roles in the field, like capturing photographs of persons attempting to defraud their spouse or the government.

But never to investigate a potential murderer, and never on her own.

After a strategy session over tea, she and Ginger had decided that the place to start was with Lizzie and her friend Abby. She found Lizzie in the kitchen, catching her before she disappeared up the servants' stairs.

The kitchen was spacious with a large wooden-topped table in the middle of the room and copper-bottomed pots and pans hanging from ceiling hooks. A gas stove, deep porcelain sink, and hefty refrigerator were well used, and Mrs. Beasley wore a path in the tiled floor between them.

Scout and Boss rushed in, Scout red in the face from whatever he and Boss had been doing outside, and both thirsty. Boss lapped up water from his bowl as Lizzie poured Scout a glass of ginger beer. Mrs. Beasley, who had never fully adapted to Scout's change in station—he had once been her helper in the kitchen, and now she waited on him—barely held in a scowl on her round, doughy face.

"Lizzie," Felicia started, "if I might have a word?"

Lizzie curtsied, her expression looking troubled. "Yes, my lady."

Felicia drew the maid into the dining room, where they could speak privately. "Please don't be distressed," Felicia said. "I only have a question about your friend Abby and about what she saw at Lady Whitmore's old house."

"Oh, my lady, I shouldn't have opened my big mouth. It wasn't my place to say anything. I was only trying to cheer Mrs. Reed up with a bit of gossip."

"Mrs. Reed was delighted, so you needn't worry about that. Though we, both Mrs. Reed and I, would like to know more before we offer our condolences, you see. We wouldn't want to say anything out of turn simply because we're not privy to the family dynamics."

"Oh, all right. Perhaps Abby is due for a small break. Would you like me to check?"

"That would be terrific." Felicia knew that Mrs. Foote was out of the way, so hopefully, the other members of the Foote family wouldn't prevent Abby from leaving. "Let's meet in the garden."

FELICIA MOVED to the front of the house, getting to the tall windows of the front entrance in time to peer outside and see Lizzie disappear behind the back of the Foote residence where the staff entrance was located. While she waited, Felicia thought that perhaps her time would be best spent calling on Miss Patricia Foote and offering her condolences.

"Pippins?"

Ginger's beloved butler soon appeared with her coat draped over one arm.

"Pippins," Felicia said with a smile. "However do you do it? Are you a mind reader?"

"No, madam," Pippins said as he helped Felicia into her coat. "Certainly not. Years of service have taught me that a summons from the entry hall means one is either coming or going."

Felicia nimbly fastened the buttons and tightened

the belt around her waist. "Ah. Of course. I won't be long. Just calling in on the Foote residence."

"I'll be here to take your coat when you return."

"Thank you, Pippins."

Recent rainfall had made the slabs slippery and not wanting to tumble, Felicia took her time. At least it had stopped raining now. She had on a fur hat and thanked the heavens for that.

A long, dreary chime, suiting the family's demeanour and especially now, with death, was answered by a squirrelly-faced butler.

"Good day," Felicia started. "I'm Lady Davenport-Witt calling to offer my condolences."

"I'm afraid the master and the lady of the house are not available at the moment," the butler droned.

"And Miss Patricia Foote?" Felicia pressed. "Is she home?"

The butler ducked his chin and waved for her to step inside. Like Hartigan House, the entry of the Foote residence had a high ceiling though electric lighting hadn't replaced the hanging gas lamps. It also lacked broad and tall windows, and without an abundance of natural light, the house took on a melancholy feel.

"If you wouldn't mind waiting here, my lady," the butler said, "I'll see if Miss Foote is available."

"That would be lovely."

Soon, Miss Foote sauntered down the staircase. Though she was dressed in the required black, the style of the frock—with flowing bell-style sleeves and a layered handkerchief skirt—was more in keeping with a Coco Chanel design intended for parties rather than mourning.

"Lady Davenport-Witt," she purred. "How kind of you to call." To the butler, she snapped. "That'll be all, Humphrey."

The butler disappeared, and Felicia worked to keep the surprise off her face at Miss Foote's disregard for the family's staff. No one at Hartigan House would dare to speak to Pippins with such a tone.

"Miss Foote," Felicia started, "please forgive my intrusion. I'm here to offer my condolences, both personally and from the Reed family."

"Thank you. Mrs. Reed has already sent a card and flowers, but it's nice to have a personal visit. Can you stay for tea? I'd be grateful for the diversion. It's so dreary around here; I'm tempted to kill myself too."

This time Felicia couldn't prevent a gasp.

Miss Foote patted Felicia's arm. "Forgive me. It's just this place and everyone in it pretending that they cared about Grandfather. What I really need is a night out at a club to dispense with my nerves, but I suppose that won't be on offer for some time."

The sitting room was unbearably dark, with the

heavy, Victorian-era curtains closed. Despite its need for modernising, Felicia found the former Whitmore residence charming. Miss Foote lit a gas lamp and rang a bell.

"I'm afraid you've missed my mother and sister. Mother has taken Charlotte to see the doctor again. Poor thing gets headaches. Do have a seat."

Felicia undid the belt of her coat and unfastened the buttons. It surprised her that Humphrey hadn't offered to take her coat, but then, Miss Foote hadn't given him a chance. She casually draped it over the back of the settee before taking a chair. Miss Foote took the one beside her, a small round table between them.

A maid hurried in and curtsied, "Miss?"

Miss Foote frowned. "Where's Abby?"

"She's having a break, miss."

Miss Foote checked her watch. "At this time? Very well, Alice, you can bring us tea."

"Yes, miss." A speedy opening of the curtains followed another curtsey and then the maid quickly disappeared. Felicia got the distinct impression that the staff didn't care for the company of their employers.

Felicia leaned in and put on an air of sympathy. "I take it that you and your grandfather were close?"

Miss Foote blinked. "Why would you say that?"

"Only because you seemed offended by how others in your household had treated him."

"We all treated him that way," Miss Foote said coolly. "Including me."

"I see. I'm sorry, then, that you had an unhappy parting with the deceased." Carefully Felicia added, "Did you speak to him, at least? To say goodbye?"

"Perhaps you didn't hear that Grandfather had a heart attack. There was no warning, and therefore no time to tidy things up in that way."

Felicia was quite certain had Ginger been there, she wouldn't be bungling things so badly! Why hadn't she gone to Ginger to get advice before coming?

Thankfully, Alice arrived with the tea and placed the tray on the table between Felicia and Miss Foote, and Felicia used the time it took for her hostess to pour to get her wits about her again.

Deciding to wait for Miss Foote to speak, Felicia was rewarded.

Miss Foote sipped her tea, then crossed her leg, letting it bounce lightly. "You must think us all an unfeeling lot, Lady Davenport-Witt," she said. "It isn't true. We all feel deeply, just not love or respect. Unfortunately, Grandfather was a cantankerous and spiteful old man."

"Not all funerals are sad events, I suppose," Felicia said. "Still, it marks a change for the family."

"Indeed. Less strife, for one thing. But I mustn't flog a dead horse." She gasped, then laughed. "Forgive my poor taste in humour. It was entirely unintended."

Having been raised in a society that demanded manners and protocol, Felicia was used to being the person in the room that challenged such things, but Miss Foote had Felicia's brashness beaten in spades.

Miss Foote reached across the table and patted Felicia's arm. "Once this charade of mourning is over, we must do something fun together. I imagine your husband would frown on your going to a club with a single friend, but shopping perhaps? I've yet to visit Mrs. Reed's shop, Feathers & Flair. I've heard it's all the rage."

"I may be in danger of boasting," Felicia said, "but I have to say it's one of the best in London. Now, you must tell me about Canada. I've never been to North America."

"Haven't you? Well, you're not exactly missing out. Canada's even more in the woods than America. I suppose New York would be interesting, but Father was always so busy in parliament, we never had a chance to venture south of the border."

Attempting to steer things back to the deceased, Felicia said, "Mr. Rothwell was your mother's father? How is she? Even children with difficult parents are known to mourn their deaths."

"She's . . . fine. I think she's more distressed about

making the funeral arrangements. This wasn't exactly how she imagined re-engaging with London society."

"I see. What will your father do now that he's finished in Canada?"

"Oh, that's a sore point, but I gather he'll look after Grandfather's affairs now. It's a bone of contention between my parents. Grandfather never got over the fact that he had no male heirs, and so my father was his reluctant choice."

"Your father is inheriting everything?" Felicia asked.

"From what I understand, unless Grandfather managed to change the will without any of us knowing." Miss Foote chortled. "Now, wouldn't that be something?" She leaned in. "I heard him threaten to give Humphrey everything, just to spite us all."

Felicia gaped. "The butler?"

"Butler and Grandfather's personal valet." Miss Foote checked her watch then stared at Felicia with a look of disappointment. "I'm afraid I have another appointment."

Felicia rose and collected her coat. "Thank you for fitting me in, unannounced. Mrs. Reed is indisposed until the child comes, but if there's anything that either the staff at Hartigan House or I can do to help, please let me know."

"We most certainly will," Miss Foote said.

"Though what we need most is your good wishes to get through the next few days so we can get on with our lives."

Felicia had been so enthralled with Patricia Foote that she'd completely forgotten that she'd summoned Abby, remembering only when she saw the maid crossing the court and disappearing behind the Foote residence. She'd have to apologise to Lizzie and request another meeting later on.

8

*G*inger was pleased that Ambrosia had popped in for a visit. There had been a time when the two ladies failed to see eye to eye. Ginger suspected the dowager Lady Gold, a proud and opinionated lady, had found it difficult to accept aid from the Hartigan family in the Gold family's time of need. The help had come in the form of a bride— Ginger herself—for her grandson and the deep pockets of Ginger's father. The arranged marriage was to benefit the Hartigan family by grafting Ginger into a titled position, Lady Gold, the wife of a baron. The Hartigan family would, in turn, save the family home, Bray Manor, from financial ruin.

Ginger and Daniel had been married for five years before he died, but most of that time was spent in Boston, where they married and lived as newlyweds, and in France and Belgium during the war. Ginger had hardly known her grandmother-in-law or Felicia, her sister-in-law.

Since Ginger's return to London, and after an unfortunate incident involving a fire at Bray Manor, Ambrosia and Felicia had become Ginger's permanent guests. Over time, Ambrosia had warmed up to Ginger, forgetting, or at least choosing not to remember, the circumstances that had joined them to each other.

"I only had one child, Daniel's father, Robert," Ambrosia said as she sat in an armchair pulled close to the bed and leaned on her silver-handled walking stick, "but I remember the day of his birth like it was yesterday." She held Ginger's gaze with her large, marble-like eyes. "It won't be the most fun you've ever had, but it's only one day. Childbirth is the great equaliser in the lives of women. The Queen has to do it the same way as the peasant."

Ginger was surprised by Ambrosia's judicious social commentary. "Oh, Grandmother. At this point, I'd do anything just to have this child out of my body and to get out of bed again."

Ambrosia snorted. "Remember you said that."

Quite desperate to change the subject, Ginger asked, "Have you seen much of the Foote family since Mr. Rothwell's passing?"

"How would I see any of them?" Ambrosia flashed

Ginger a look of consternation. "Do you think I should call on them?"

"There's no need for that. Felicia has already gone on behalf of the family. I was just wondering if you'd heard anything."

"It's a little early for funeral arrangements to be announced." Ambrosia sighed. "It's been a while since I've been to a good funeral."

"Grandmother!"

"It's true. At my age, one has to get ideas and begin preparations. One can't just leave things for one's children to do. One never knows what they might say!"

Ginger laughed. "Rest assured, we'd only have kind things to say about you. But enough of that. You'll be around for a long time yet." Ambrosia was too proud and feisty to go down without a fight, of that Ginger was certain.

"And how is Mrs. Schofield?"

"Ginger, you're talking like you've been out of the country for weeks. Mrs. Schofield is as loquacious today as she was yesterday."

"I just thought perhaps you'd wish to visit her again."

Ambrosia narrowed her deeply wrinkled eyes. "What are you up to, Ginger? I can tell you want something from me. Just come out and say it."

"Very well. I have reason to believe that perhaps

Mr. Rothwell's death wasn't due to natural causes, and since I obviously can't ask around myself . . ."

Ambrosia's lips twitched into a rare smile. "You really must be dreadfully bored to come up with something like that. Mr. Rothwell was an old man. Old men just pass away sometimes."

"He wasn't that much older than you," Ginger protested.

"Yes, but he was in ill health, as was evidenced by the wheelchair he depended on. I am only in need of this walking stick for balance, though I admit, the staircase seems to be getting longer with time."

Ginger was alarmed. "Are they too difficult? We could move you into the study downstairs if you prefer. I can work from the library or set a new office up here, just as easily."

Ambrosia flapped a hand, the jewels of her rings catching the lamplight. "I'm not about to fall down them yet. Now, if I were to see Mrs. Schofield, what exactly would you like to know?"

"Anything she might know about the Foote family members."

"If anyone would know, it would be Mrs. Schofield," Ambrosia said. "Now that Lady Whitmore has moved away, Mrs. Schofield is the queen of gossip in Mallowan Court." She shifted in her chair, leaned on her walking stick, and hoisted herself onto her feet.

"You don't mind if I have a little lie-down before I begin my reconnaissance mission?"

Ginger smiled. "Of course not."

Nature was calling on Ginger once again, an annoyance to be sure, but at least it gave her a chance to look out of the window herself. She was in time to witness Felicia leaving the Foote residence and briskly walking across the court. A motorcar drove up—the green Morgan—and parked, Miss Foote's young man inside.

"Is that Miss Patricia Foote?" Ambrosia said, stepping in beside Ginger.

"It is."

Miss Foote ran, rather energetically, to the motorcar.

Ambrosia harrumphed. "Miss Foote certainly seems happy for a young lady who's just lost her grandfather."

Before Ginger had finished saying goodbye to Ambrosia, Felicia breezed into the room, nearly knocking into the elder lady.

"Felicia!" Ambrosia sputtered. "Do watch where you're going, child."

Ginger stiffened. Felicia and Ambrosia had a tinder-box-style relationship, and Ginger was certain Felicia would ruffle at being called a child, especially now that she was a married lady. Still, to Ginger's infinite surprise, Felicia embraced her grandmother in a full-body hug.

"Oh, Grandmama."

Ambrosia stared at her granddaughter with a rare look of confusion. "Pray tell what has brought this on."

Felicia dropped her coat and gloves on an empty chair. "I've just come from the most peculiar meeting with Miss Patricia Foote. She has absolutely no sense of loss from the death of her grandfather. It's like she's glad he's gone."

Felicia tilted her head and looked at Ambrosia fondly. "I know I've been a pain for you to bring up, but I do appreciate the effort you put in, and I would be shattered if you left me."

Ambrosia reached for Felicia's fine-boned hand—the elder's a marked difference with large blue veins and knobby knuckles—and squeezed.

Ginger's eyes teared up. They did that more often since she'd been with child, and she discreetly reached for a handkerchief on her side table and dabbed at her eyes.

"You must tell us all about what you've learned," Ginger said.

Ambrosia, who seemed to be revived and forgetting her plans to lie down said, "I'll ring for tea."

With both armchairs tucked in close to the bed and

a table topped with a tea tray between them, Ginger prompted Felicia to begin her account.

"According to Miss Foote," Felicia started, "she wasn't the only one who disliked Mr. Rothwell. Apparently, it was a sentiment shared by every member of the family."

Ambrosia snorted. "That's hardly evidence of a murderous plot. He was aged and infirm. It was only a matter of time before nature would've taken its course."

"Oh, Grandmama," Felicia said. "I do hate it when you speak that way."

"It's the way life works, Felicia. No one lives forever." She turned to Ginger. "You never mentioned what caused feelings of suspicion to arise."

"As chance would have it, Lizzie's friend works as a maid for the Foote family. She reported seeing every family member visiting Mr. Rothwell, one by one, the morning he died, and that on every occasion, muffled arguing was heard."

Ambrosia looked displeased. "This Abby is hardly exercising discretion."

Ginger couldn't disagree but offered this rationale. "She confided in Lizzie because she knows Lizzie works for me."

"Miss Patricia Foote's statements support Abby's

observation," Felicia said. "According to Miss Foote, none of the family members liked Mr. Rothwell."

"Did she say why?" Ginger asked.

"Only that he was cantankerous and spiteful."

"I wonder why he turned so sour?" Ginger mused. "Did she mention her parents? How are they dealing with Mr. Rothwell's death?"

"Mrs. Foote is eager to get the funeral over with," Felicia said. "She did leave in a hurry earlier on. I'm beginning to wonder if she's been planning this funeral for a while."

"I'm assuming she's in line to inherit," Ginger said.

Felicia shook her head. "Not according to Miss Foote. It seems Mr. Rothwell believed firmly in the patriarch and that inheritances should go through a male heir."

"And there isn't one?" Ambrosia asked.

"Miss Foote said her grandfather was passing everything on to her father."

"It comes to motive," Ginger said. "If Mr. Foote was to inherit, perhaps he was eager to get his hands on the money. I wonder what his financial situation is like." She turned to Felicia. "Perhaps you could ask Charles what he knows? From his duties at the House of Commons, I would assume he's acquainted with Mr. Foote's former employer Lord Byng."

"I could ask," Felicia said. "Mr. Foote seems like

the prime suspect. Though, there's also Humphrey, the butler, who was also Mr. Rothwell's valet."

Ginger pushed a lock of red hair that had fallen from its pin behind her ear. "We mustn't discount the ladies in the family."

"What motive would Mrs. Foote have?" Felicia asked.

"It could be anything. Perhaps, unbeknownst to her husband, she'd convinced her father to change his will, and he was threatening to change it back."

"Speak of the devil," Felicia said, looking out the window. "The Foote motorcar has returned. Mrs. Foote and Miss Charlotte have exited and look as unhappy as ever."

Ambrosia stifled a yawn. "This time, I really am going to have a lie-down. Felicia, can you ring for Langley and tell her I'd like my bed turned down?" She got to her feet but paused at the door. "I think you're on a fool's errand, Ginger, but I'll play along. I'll arrange to have tea with Mrs. Schofield tomorrow."

"Thank you, Grandmother," Ginger said. "You're a brick."

"Georgia," Ambrosia returned with a frown, using Ginger's birth name. "Must you be so vulgar?"

Once she'd left and the tapping of her walking stick quieted down the corridor, both Ginger and Felicia broke out in laughter.

"There's no one else like her," Felicia said as she rang the bell for Ambrosia's maid.

Ginger couldn't agree more. "There certainly isn't."

Felicia slipped into her coat and began feeding her fingers into her gloves. "I must head off too. Charles will be home soon. I'll be sure to ask about Lord Byng and Mr. Foote."

"Did Miss Foote say anything about the young man that motors up to collect her?" Ginger asked.

"No, but she did end our time together rather abruptly," Felicia said. "I was barely at the front door here when she scampered out to meet him."

"I'm rather curious about who he might be," Ginger said. "And why it seems he never enters the house. It's as if he's not welcome."

Felicia removed a piece of paper from her pocket. "I'm curious too," she said with a smile. "It's why I jotted down the number on his number plate."

Ginger laughed. "I've trained you well. Now all I have to do is convince Basil to check the records. I'm afraid he's not as willing to entertain nefarious possibilities when it comes to our neighbour's sudden demise."

As Felicia made to leave, Ginger said, "Give Charles my love."

"And you, Basil."

"I will, and on second thoughts, perhaps you could

accompany Ambrosia to tea with Mrs. Schofield." Ginger added, "As they say, two heads are better than one."

"Any other time, I'd flatly refuse," Felicia said with a scoff, "but I'll do it for the sake of justice."

Ginger chuckled at Felicia's dramatic exit. Then, alone in her room, she allowed herself to sink deeply into her pillows. She closed her eyes, but her mind wouldn't rest. There was just something about the whole matter that didn't sit right with her.

But perhaps Ambrosia was right, and Ginger was just a bored expectant mother with an active imagination. Everyone grieved in their own way, the Foote family included. It was unscrupulous of her to entertain accusations of malice.

The best thing to do now was to sleep on things, which was precisely what she did.

9

*G*inger was roused later that afternoon by a damp nose and doggy breath.

"Bossy!" she said with a smile as she pushed his perpetually happy face away from hers. After shifting into a seated position, she proceeded to give Boss the love he deserved, scratching him behind the ears.

The door pushed open wider, and Scout strolled in. A shadow of fuzz was on his lip that never used to be there, Ginger noted with a shock. Scout, thin and lanky with knee-knobby legs, settled into one of the armchairs. "Hello, Mum." He glanced about the room. "You must be bored having to stay in here all the time."

"It's not so bad," Ginger said. "Aunt Felicia and Lady Gold visit me. And Boss. And now you. How's your day gone? Did your studies with Mr. Fulton go well?"

Scout nodded. "I'm learning about horse breeding. It's big business in England, and Mr. Fulton says I should start thinking about what I want to do for a living. And I already know what I want to do, Mum. I want to own and race horses."

Scout's interest in horses was nothing new. She and Basil were independently wealthy and worked not because they needed to but because they followed a calling. It appeared that Scout had found his calling as well.

Ginger watched her son as he spoke, her chest full of pride. Scout had come a long way from the little waif she'd met on the SS *Rosa* who could hardly read or write and habitually dropped his *H*s.

An extended pause between them also reminded Ginger how Scout had grown quieter and more pensive in recent months, and she found she missed his childish and talkative ways.

Braxton Hicks gripped her, and she stiffened as she gripped her belly. Scout stared at her with alarm. "Are you all right, Mum?"

"I'm fine. The baby's just practising, getting ready for his or her big day."

Scout swallowed then said, "The baby will change things."

Ginger could hear the words left unspoken. *Between us.*

"Certainly, some things will change, Scout, but not all things. You will be a big brother, and I shall have a baby. However, you will still be my son, and I shall still be your mother."

By the way Scout's eyes softened, Ginger knew it was the right thing to say.

Scout stood, stuffing his fists into his trousers, and for a moment, Ginger feared he would leave, but instead, he moved towards the window. The new family across the court was certainly an attraction for everyone, it seemed.

"Are you looking for Charlotte?"

Scout spun on his heel. "No," he said, a little too forcefully for the occasion. The blush that crept up his neck suggested otherwise. "Why would you say that?"

"It's normal for a boy your age to become interested in girls, Scout. You can ask Dad about it."

Scout pressed his lips together, his eyes gazing upwards as if he was making a decision. Ginger hoped he'd confide in her and let out a slow breath when he did.

"I think she's pretty. And she has a nice cat."

"Perhaps one day you'll have a chance to speak to her."

Scout blinked back with interest. "What should I say?"

"You could start by telling her your name and asking for hers."

"But I already know her name."

"She doesn't know that. But if you'd rather, you could ask for her cat's name. Then introduce her to Boss."

On hearing his name, Boss raised his chin off his paws from his position on the bed.

"Isn't this a bad time, with her grandfather dead?"

"It depends," Ginger said. "Perhaps she could use a friend to talk to. She's only just returned to London from Canada. I doubt she has many friends here yet."

Scout seemed uncertain and turned back to the window. Then he spun to face Ginger. "She's outside now! Should I go?"

Ginger smiled. "Yes, go."

TRAYS OF ROAST lamb with mint sauce accompanied by roast potatoes and carrots had been brought up by Lizzie and Grace, and Ginger ate with Basil in their bedroom. Basil pushed the table where he sat to the bed while Ginger kept to the bed with her tray.

"How was your day?" Basil enquired.

"I'm frightfully tired of these four walls," Ginger

said. "I'm beginning to feel like a prisoner in my own home."

Basil patted her hand. "It'll be worth it in the end, love. I understand Felicia and Ambrosia have been to see you."

"If it weren't for the new neighbours, I don't know what we'd talk about. Everyone is quite interested in the cause of Mr. Rothwell's death."

Basil stilled, his fork hovering in the air. "I don't understand. Dr. Longden said he had a heart attack."

"Yes, well, a rumour has been going around the staff that perhaps there was more to it than that."

Basil's lips twitched with humour. "A rumour? What a lovely diversion for you."

Ginger smirked in response. "Felicia met with Miss Patricia Foote—" as Basil raised a brow, she quickly added, "—to offer our condolences, and Felicia's account of the affair was intriguing."

"In what fashion?" Basil asked.

"Apparently, no one in the family was fond of the man. Miss Foote showed no sadness whatsoever."

"It wouldn't be the first time that a family was relieved to have a difficult family member gone. It doesn't mean anything crooked has happened."

"Lizzie's friend happens to be a maid employed by the Foote family, and she told Lizzie that each member, on their own, visited Mr. Rothwell on the morning he died and that each encounter resulted in angry outbursts."

Basil patted his mouth with a napkin. "Might I assume that you've finished the mystery book by Agatha Christie? Your imagination at the moment is fascinating."

"I'm pleased that you are entertained," Ginger said stiffly. "And no, I've not quite finished it. I'm sleeping a lot more these days."

Basil smiled. "Oh, don't be angry, love. For the sake of argument, list the motives. I'm certain you've thought this through."

"Actually, I have," Ginger admitted, "though what I have on offer is limited. Miss Foote revealed to Felicia that Mr. Rothwell intended for Mr. Archibald Foote to be his sole heir. Apparently, he's a believer in passing down solely through the male line. Mr. Foote either needed the money now and couldn't wait for a natural passing, or he was worried that Mr. Rothwell had changed his mind about his convictions and was going to change the will.

"Mrs. Foote, knowing that her husband was going to get everything anyway, pushed things along because she just couldn't bear her father's grumpy demeanour. Or, if her father had changed the will in her favour, was afraid he might change it back.

"Miss Patricia Foote, well, I haven't come up with a

compelling motive for her, except that perhaps, since Mr. Rothwell held the family purse strings—apparently Mr. Foote hasn't got a hefty bank account of his own—he was threatening to cut her off. She's been seen with a young man who's not darkened the door of the Foote residence, so one might assume he wasn't acceptable to Mr. Rothwell."

Basil cut in. "Or other members of the family. Have you learned from your gossip mill the name of this mystery man?"

"No, but Felicia did get his car number plate."

"I see."

Basil's grin annoyed Ginger, and she pointed her fork at him. "You're patronising me."

"I'm not, I'm not," Basil returned with a laugh. "I'm enthralled. Please do continue."

"That's all I have," Ginger said.

"What about Lizzie's family friend?"

Ginger hadn't considered Abby in this scenario. "I certainly hope not. But Felicia says the butler, who was also Mr. Rothwell's valet, might have inherited. Valets become privy to all kinds of intimacies. Perhaps he knows something." Ginger wiggled her fingers. "Listen to me prattle on. You must tell me about your day. Anything of interest happen at the Yard?"

"Not at Scotland Yard, per se. It turns out our good

neighbour, Mr. Foote, reported a suspicious breaking and entering to the local police."

"Is that so?" Ginger sat up straighter. "And how did you find out about it?"

"I'd put out a memo to be personally informed if anything involving the Foote family came to the attention of the police," Basil said. "I went to the local police station to talk to the officer who took the call, but by then, Mr. Foote had rung again, saying it was a misunderstanding."

"How curious." When the Foote family had moved onto Mallowan Court, Ginger had no idea they'd be so dramatic. "Perhaps he acted out a threat to that mysterious young man with whom Miss Patricia Foote is keeping company, but hadn't the courage to follow through."

"Perhaps, but that's not even the interesting part," Basil added with a grin. "While I was there, a little old lady came in. She was about Scout's height. This might interest your fashion sense—she had strands of blue-grey hair poking out from under a fur-trimmed hat." He smiled. "Anyway, she marched in like she owned the place, and I could tell the poor constable who waited on her had a tough time keeping a straight face."

"She sounds like quite a character," Ginger said.

"Indeed. She went on to report an unruly neighbour—I learned afterwards she's in an ongoing feud.

My attention was captured when I overheard the constable in charge reciting her name. 'Mrs. Neville Rothwell'."

"Such a coincidence!" Ginger didn't bother hiding her surprise. "Don't tell me she's related to our dead neighbour."

"Indeed she is," Basil said. "After overhearing her last name, I had to enquire. They're related through marriage. She's the sister of Crispin Rothwell's late wife as well as the sister-in-law of his late brother. You see, two sisters had married two brothers. Her husband, Neville Rothwell, has been gone for some time."

A lock of red hair had fallen over Ginger's eyes, and she pushed it back behind her ear. "Did she know of Mr. Crispin Rothwell's death?"

"Apparently not. And I have to say I was shocked by her response when she heard the news. She laughed so loudly, everyone in the station stopped to stare."

Ginger smiled at the image. "Did she tell you what was so funny?"

"Oh indeed, she did. She couldn't wait to tell me how the scoundrel had finally got his just desserts."

"I don't doubt Mr. Crispin Rothwell was capable of misdeeds," Ginger said. "Do go on."

"Mrs. Neville Rothwell is the middle one of three sisters; she referred to the youngest as Mrs. Joseph Entwistle, now deceased, though the three sisters were all alive when their parents died. It turns out that their inheritance wasn't distributed evenly between the three sisters, with the older sister getting the lion's share."

"The late Mrs. Crispin Rothwell."

"As Mrs. Neville Rothwell put it, Crispin Rothwell had swindled her family out of their money when he married their older sister, beguiling her with lies."

"Wouldn't Crispin Rothwell have a right to his wife's money?"

"He would. Mrs. Crispin Rothwell had promised to divide her share of the fortune between the two remaining sisters when she died, and that Crispin Rothwell would see to it."

"Ah," Ginger said with understanding. "And in the end, Crispin Rothwell decided not to share."

10

After a restless night—partly because of the baby moving about and partly because her mind couldn't let go of a possible murder event across the court—Ginger asked Lizzie if she could arrange for Abby to see her.

Lizzie, who'd finished pouring Ginger a cup of coffee, raised a brow. "Here? In your room?"

"I don't see how we can do it otherwise. Mr. Reed would be deeply disappointed if I left this room for any reason other than when nature calls, and I really do want to hear Abby's concerns regarding Mr. Rothwell from her own mouth."

"Very well," Lizzie said. "She takes a morning break. I'll see if she can come."

"Do ask her to be discreet," Ginger said. "For her

sake as well as ours. I wouldn't want Mrs. Foote to think we're attempting to poach her staff from her."

"Of course, madam." Lizzie curtsied, then left the room.

Ginger spent the time eating breakfast while reading the front page of the newspaper. By the time she'd finished her toast and coffee, Basil had kissed her goodbye for the day, Ambrosia had confirmed a time for tea with Mrs. Schofield for later that afternoon, and Scout had wished her a good day before starting his studies with Mr. Fulton.

When Lizzie reappeared to collect the dirty dishes and empty coffee carafe, she had Abby in tow.

"Madam," Lizzie started, "this is Abby, Mrs. Foote's maid."

Despite the laugh lines around the maid's mouth, evidence of Lizzie's attribute of cheeriness, and her dark, intelligent eyes, Abby Green looked like the sort who'd seen it all. She was Ginger's height but far curvier than modern fashion trends gave room for. Her hands, clasped in front of her, looked red and well used. She curtsied. "Good morning, madam."

"Good morning, Miss Green," Ginger said warmly. "I do thank you for coming to see me. I realise it's rather an odd request."

Abby simply nodded.

Lizzie, who seemed to work in slow motion,

smoothed out the sheets around Ginger's feet, then carefully picked up the tray. Once Lizzie had closed the door behind her, Ginger said, "I won't keep you, Abby. I know you have work to do and don't want to be missed, so please accept my gratitude for using your well-earned break to come to see me."

Abby dipped at the knees at the acknowledgement.

"It's my pleasure, madam. Lizzie told me why you sent for me. I just don't know if I can tell you more than I've already told her."

"Do you know that I operate an investigative office?"

"Yes, madam."

"This is why my curiosity is piqued, and I admit, I might be a little restless—" She waved a hand over the obvious mound under her quilt, "while waiting. So, please indulge me with a retelling."

"Very well, madam. I work for Mrs. Foote, not as a lady's maid mind—she doesn't like maids to get into her personal things, but I'm her preference for cleaning her room and organising her wardrobes and such things. I was dusting in her room, which is just across the corridor from Mr. Rothwell's bedroom. I don't know if she forgot that I was there, but I could hear her and Mr. Rothwell arguing."

"Did you hear what was said?" Ginger asked.

"Not clearly. Something about finally letting go

and giving up. She slammed Mr. Rothwell's door then ran down the staircase." At Ginger's look, Abby added, "Their raised voices caused me to stop what I was doing, and I went to the door to look in the corridor. I ducked back when Mrs. Foote stormed out of her father's room, so she didn't see me."

"What happened next?"

"I went back to dusting—the door was opened a crack—and next thing I saw was Mr. Foote going into Mr. Rothwell's room without knocking."

"And they argued as well?"

"Yes, madam. All I could make out was that Mr. Foote said he was doing all he could."

"Could about what?" Ginger asked.

"I can hardly say, madam, but if I were to guess, I'd say it had to do with Miss Foote and her fellow."

"And who visited Mr. Foote after that? Miss Patricia Foote?"

"Yes, madam. She shouted the loudest of them all. I can't repeat the words she said, but so they were so shocking to hear, coming out of the mouth of a young lady and directed at her elder."

"Did any of the staff go in after that? Mr. Humphrey perhaps?" Ginger asked. "I understand he also worked as Mr. Rothwell's valet."

"Not that I saw, madam. Only—" For the first time, Abby hesitated in her retelling.

"Only?" Ginger prompted.

"Miss Charlotte went in next, madam."

Ginger tilted her head in question. "Don't tell me she argued with Mr. Rothwell as well?"

"No, but I'll tell you, her face? All scrunched up like she'd eaten a lemon, and she slammed the door so hard, I couldn't believe the strength that came from that little girl."

Mr. Rothwell had quite a parade of visitors. "Anyone else?" Ginger asked.

"I was behind in my work at that point," Abby said, "so I really put my nose to it. If someone else called on Mr. Rothwell before he died, I didn't see it."

"Very good," Ginger said. "Thank you for coming, Miss Green."

Abby glanced up from under short eyelashes as she smoothed out her maid's apron. "If Mrs. Foote should ever find out I was here—"

"She'll never hear about it from me or anyone in this house, I can assure you. You did the right thing by coming. Now you mustn't worry about it any longer."

"Yes, madam."

Abby curtsied, then left. Ginger imagined the maid using sturdy, long strides down the corridor to the narrow staff staircase at the end, exiting through the kitchen and back garden, and circling to the staff entrance of the Foote residence.

The situation the maid had relayed was hardly proof of foul play, but it was most certainly curious. In Ginger's mind, there was no doubt that the Foote family was eager for the disagreeable Mr. Rothwell to leave this earth. The question was, could one of them actually have hurried his journey along? And if so, which one?

11

*P*ippins arrived with a pleasant announcement. "Mrs. Hill is calling, madam," he said.

"Oh, do send her up!"

Matilda Hill had once been a student at the London Medical School for Women along with Ginger's good friend Haley Higgins, when, unfortunately, circumstances forced her to drop out early. Instead, she had married another good friend of Ginger's, the Reverend Oliver Hill, and the two now shared a beautiful infant daughter. As a service to members of their congregation, Matilda assisted as a midwife, putting her medical knowledge to good use.

Matilda entered with the confidence that a lady in good standing with her family, church, and society would possess, but with none of the hubris that often went with it. Dressed in a simple cotton frock, Matilda glowed—her heart-shaped face brightened when she laid eyes on Ginger, and her bow-shaped lips tugged into a warm smile.

"Ginger, darling, how are you holding up?"

They embraced rather awkwardly; Matilda leaned down and reached around Ginger's shoulders as Ginger sat upright in her bed. Claiming an empty chair, Matilda said, "I heard that Dr. Longden had put you on bed rest. You must be dreadfully bored."

"You can't imagine."

"Oh, believe me, I can," Matilda said with a laugh. "It was only seven months ago that I was in the same position as you, but take my advice and enjoy this time of rest, peace, and quiet."

"Indeed I should," Ginger said. "How is little Margaret?"

"A delight and a terror wrapped up in one. It helps to have so many in the congregation willing to help out."

Ginger was reminded about her uncompleted task regarding finding a new nanny. She really must get back to that, and now, with nothing much to do but nose into a family's affairs which were not her business, it would behove her to use this time to resume that.

However, she kept these thoughts to herself, as not

everyone, like the Hills, was in a position to employ a nanny.

They chatted about infant care and moved on to the health and well-being of their husbands before Matilda enquired about the new neighbours. "I've heard they've had a death there already."

"News travels fast in London," Ginger said.

"Oliver spotted the obituary in the newspaper and noticed the address on Mallowan Court," Matilda said. "The Foote family isn't part of our congregation, but I should like to send condolences, anyway."

"I'm sure they would appreciate it."

"I promised Oliver I wouldn't be out too long. Margaret's getting a tooth, and she's none too happy about it." Matilda took Ginger's hand and squeezed. "But if there's anything I can do for you, you be sure to let me know." She kissed Ginger on both cheeks, pausing at the door to finger wave. "This too shall pass," she said brightly before disappearing.

Ginger mused about her friend and how radiant she appeared. Motherhood certainly looked good on Matilda, and Ginger took comfort that the same would be true for her.

. . .

GINGER WAS BEGINNING to feel like her bedroom was busier than Waterloo Station as Felicia arrived on the heels of Matilda Hill.

"I came in time to go to tea with Grandmama and Mrs. Schofield," Felicia announced. With eager eyes, she enquired, "Have you learned anything new since yesterday?"

"The maid Abby was here, brought in by Lizzie," Ginger said.

"Oh, boo." Felicia sat and crossed her legs. "I'm disappointed I missed her. What did she have to say?"

Ginger filled Felicia in on Abby's report. "It seems that there was no love lost between any member of the Foote family and the deceased. Did you gather any information on Lord Byng regarding Archibald Foote?"

"None at all. Charles didn't even know Mr. Foote by name. He says he doesn't keep track of everyone's secretaries unless necessary."

Ginger rested her head on the back of her pillow. "It feels like we're chasing our tails."

"It's something to do until the baby comes."

Ginger squinted at her former sister-in-law. "I'm surprised you don't have plenty to do as Lady of Witt House." Ginger thought Felicia was spending more time at Hartigan House now than she had when she lived there.

"It ran quite well before I came," Felicia said with a

sniff. "All my friends are still going to clubs and chasing young men. I can't very well do that anymore. And Witt House is large and rather overwhelming. I feel alone in my own house when Charles isn't there to keep me company."

Felicia was still adapting to the big change in her life, and Ginger thought her feelings about Witt House would change when her children started coming.

"You know you're always welcome here, Felicia," Ginger said kindly. "And I do appreciate the company."

"Good." Felicia got to her feet, holding her handbag over her forearm. "I must find Grandmama. I do hope Mrs. Schofield has something juicy to share."

ONCE QUIET DESCENDED, Ginger took Matilda's admonition to heart and returned to reading her book. Despite the well-crafted writing—Mrs. Christie was brilliant in that regard—Ginger found her eyelids grew heavy and allowed herself to enjoy a light slumber. That was until Lizzie's arrival startled her awake.

With a red face and a quick curtsey, Lizzie blurted, "Madam, excuse me, but I thought you'd like to know."

Ginger was immediately concerned. Lizzie was usually cheerful and light-footed. Her storming in with a look of distress was quite uncharacteristic of her. "Lizzie, what is it?"

"I was at the Foote residence asking Mrs. Garner, the cook, if I could speak to Abby when she came in. She'd found a cushion in the fireplace in Mr. Rothwell's room, madam. It was charred along one side, but the piece saved clearly had a bloodstain in the middle of it."

"Yes," Ginger said carefully. It wouldn't be unusual to discard a stained cushion, although one would be more apt to put it into the rag bag than the fireplace.

"Abby was as white as a sheet. She said she recognised the cushion—it was hand-stitched with Mr. Rothwell's initials—I saw it with my own eyes as she held it up with pinched fingers. She said it was one of Mr. Rothwell's special cushions, and when she helped to make the bed after they'd taken the body away, she couldn't find it. It wasn't until she took a good look at the fireplace that she saw the cushion tucked in behind the grate."

"Behind the grate?"

"Yes, madam. Whoever threw it in missed the coals, the cushion hitting the bricks at the back and sliding behind the grate. Still close enough to burn the edges, but not enough to ignite and destroy the cushion."

The attempt to discard the small cushion in such a

fashion raised Ginger's suspicions—something was amiss.

"Mrs. Garner questioned the staff," Lizzie continued, "even as I stood right there, like she'd forgotten about me, and they all denied ever seeing the cushion or knowing how the blood got there. Humphrey and Mrs. Garner got into a row. He wanted to leave well enough alone, saying it would only bring unwanted attention to the family, but Mrs. Garner thought the police should be called. What if someone had broken into the house and killed Mr. Rothwell in his sleep!"

Alert now, Ginger sat up straight and leaned towards her maid. "What happened next?"

"Abby disappeared while Humphrey and Mrs. Garner were having words. When she returned, she announced to everyone that she'd called the police— she's that kind," Lizzie interjected, "she'll do the right thing, even if it cost her her job." Her round brown eyes latched on to Ginger. "Madam, you could've heard a pin drop."

elicia linked arms with her grandmother as they made the short trek to the house next door. Though the rain had thinned into a fine mist, Felicia wouldn't chance that Grandmama might slip, her walking cane notwithstanding.

Though only a married lady for a month, Felicia couldn't help but notice the change in Grandmama's demeanour when it came to her only granddaughter. Gone were the seemingly near-hysterics that radiated at the surface of the older lady's emotions—and Felicia admitted she was guilty of stirring up her grandmother's ire, sometimes intentionally—to be replaced with an uncharacteristic calm, as if a burden had been lifted and was now carried by another.

Felicia held in the huff she felt at the realisation. Had she really been a burden to her grandmother all these years? She jolly well hoped not. And if so, she would make amends now by being a helpful and responsible member of the family.

The long doorbell tone at the Schofield residence was answered by Mrs Schofield's maid Lucy, who naturally recognised them.

"Mrs. Schofield is expecting us," Grandmama said.

"Yes, madam," the maid said. "She's waiting in the sitting room."

After relieving the ladies of their coats, the maid led the way to Mrs. Schofield, who awaited them. "Lady Gold and Lady Davenport-Witt, madam," Lucy properly announced.

Mrs. Schofield stood to greet them. Her pure-white hair had yet to meet the scissors of the modern age and was tied into a bun on the top of her head.

"Hello, ladies," she said, her thin bony fingers playing with a long string of beads. "Do come in. I'm honoured to have the pleasure of having tea with two prestigious ladies such as yourselves."

Ambrosia nodded as if Mrs. Schofield's platitudes were the least that she expected and took a seat near the fireplace.

"Thank you for having us," Felicia said as she removed her white-leather gloves. "Novembers can be so dreary. We need our friends to cheer us, don't we, Mrs. Schofield?"

"Indeed."

Lucy returned with the tea tray, leaving it for Mrs. Schofield to do the pouring.

Felicia gazed out the window rather pointedly. "I've had the privilege of having tea with the new neighbours, Mrs. Foote and Miss Patricia Foote, to be precise, before they were hit with tragedy. I paid my respects after the fact but only had the opportunity to speak to Miss Foote. Have you met them, Mrs. Schofield?"

"Sadly, no." Mrs. Schofield sipped her tea, glanced at Grandmama, then added, "You must tell me your impressions, Lady Gold."

Grandmama's nose slanted upward in a way Felicia had witnessed thousands of times, like a bird who got the worm and was about to express insincere regrets about not having shared it. "I don't wish to speak ill of the bereaved," Grandmama said.

"I'm not surprised to hear they were downcast," Mrs. Schofield said, nodding towards the street-side windows. "I couldn't help witnessing a rather troubling discourse on the pavement—Lucy had left the window open, silly girl. So I heard everything."

With a smug grin, Mrs. Schofield sipped her tea, forcing Felicia and Ambrosia to wait in suspense. Felicia goaded, "Mrs. Schofield, I'm sure you accidentally heard nothing of interest."

It was precisely the response the elderly widow was hoping for if one could go by the gleam that twinkled in her watery blue eyes.

"I'll allow you to decide for yourselves," she said. "The conversation in question took place between Miss Foote, the elder, and a young gentleman driving an old type of motorcar. Miss Foote was upset, not with the young man, as I could see through the crack in the curtains that he had his arm about her shoulders. Miss Foote pronounced to her gentleman that her grandfather, the late Mr. Rothwell, had threatened to cut off her allowance, and because of that, she couldn't marry the young man."

"She was engaged?" Felicia said.

Mrs. Schofield offered a sly look. "Perhaps she still is. The young man—she called him Murray—refused to accept the prospect of breaking off the betrothal. He told Miss Foote to give it time—that things would work out."

13

The charred and bloodied cushion had been collected and filed away by a member of the Metropolitan Police.

Ginger and Basil discussed the situation as they dined together once again—Ginger with a tray in bed and Basil at the table he'd dragged next to it.

"On its own, it's not evidence of a misdeed,' Basil said. "Dr. Longden stated that it wasn't uncommon for a man Mr. Rothwell's age to rupture a vessel in his nose. Perhaps it happened before the heart attack."

Boss, smelling the food, jumped onto the bed. Ginger held him at arm's length and signed for him to lie down. She'd taught the bright dog to respond to nonverbal commands when he was a puppy, and the effort had come in handy many times. She returned her attention to Basil.

"Why then was it thrown into the fire? According to Lizzie, who saw it first-hand, it was delicately monogrammed with Mr. Rothwell's initials. It would be hard to replace before someone noticed it was gone."

Basil shrugged. "Destroying it would be easier than cleaning it, I suppose."

"Proper laundering could've saved the cushion, Basil. Any trained staff member would know that." Boss nudged Ginger's leg and stared up with hopeful brown eyes. "I find the placement of the stain suspicious," Ginger continued. "Right in the middle, as if someone had aimed for his nose and held the cushion tightly."

Basil's hazel eyes wrinkled at the corners as he considered her. "Normally, I wouldn't put much into a bit of blood on a cushion, but you make rather good points. I'll speak to Morris in the morning and dig around a bit more."

Ginger held little trust in Superintendent Morris' instincts, but she kept her feelings of disdain to herself. She and Basil agreed when it came to their opinions of the man, but he was Basil's superior, and there was nothing either of them could do about that.

After a second nudge by Boss, who was being undeniably adorable, Ginger slipped him a piece of lamb, allowing him to clean the gravy off her fingers.

"I do believe the animal gets fed well in the kitchen."

"I'm not feeding him because I think he's hungry. I want him to know that he's still important to me." She patted her stomach. "I'd hate for there to be ill will between them."

Basil laughed. "He's a dog, Ginger, and a happy one at that. I doubt he'll feel anything but the strange desire to lick our baby's face."

Ginger and Basil sat up when Felicia, with a glint of excitement in her eyes, breezed into the room. "Good, you're here."

Ginger pointed at her belly. "Where else would I be, darling?"

Felicia perched on the corner of the bed as she removed the silk scarf wrapped around her neck. "I mean Basil. And you, of course. Grandmama and I have just returned from having tea with Mrs. Schofield. That lady is an amazing fount of information."

"You mean gossip," Basil said wryly.

"What have you learned?" Ginger asked.

"The first name of the man who drives the Morgan. He's called Murray, and he's Miss Patricia Foote's fiancé!"

Ginger ducked her chin. "How peculiar that Mrs.

Foote didn't say so when she and her daughter were over."

"Unless it's a recent event," Basil said.

"There was less than twenty-four hours between their visit and the death of Mr. Rothwell. Hardly a convenient time to propose."

"But not impossible," Basil said. "Some blokes have a very poor sense of timing."

"I can shed light on your debate," Felicia said. "According to Mrs. Schofield, the couple have been engaged for some time and Mr. Rothwell disapproved. He'd threatened to cut Miss Foote's allowance if she didn't break it off."

Ginger hummed. "That would be motive. For either Miss Foote or her fellow."

"This is the same motorcar you asked me about, Ginger? The 1922 Darmont-Morgan?"

"Yes, it is."

Basil pulled a folded piece of paper from his shirt pocket. "Braxton handed me this as I left the Yard today. It's the name of the man who owns the car of that registration number. A Mr. Murray Entwistle."

"So now we know his name," Felicia said. "Should we see what we can find out about him?"

Ginger's lips twitched at the word "we". Felicia had brought herself into the investigation even before Basil had.

To Basil, she said, "Entwistle. Wasn't that the name of the lady who you mentioned earlier, the youngest sister of Mr. Rothwell's late wife?"

"Indeed," Basil said.

Ginger reached for Basil's arm. "Basil love, I'd like to see the newspaper from the day Mr. Rothwell died. There should be a copy in the library."

"Certainly, darling."

As Basil made the short journey down the corridor to the library, Felicia narrowed her gaze at Ginger. "Are you thinking what I'm thinking?"

"Perhaps," Ginger said with a sly grin. "What are you thinking?"

"That something in the newspaper angered Mr. Rothwell so much that it triggered the succession of arguments with his family members."

"Very good," Ginger said.

Basil returned with a paper and handed it, open to the society pages, to Ginger. "I found it."

Ginger's eye went to the small announcement at the bottom of the page. "Mr. Murray Entwistle would like to announce his engagement to Miss Patricia Foote," Ginger read aloud. "Details to follow."

Felicia whistled. "Now what?"

Basil headed for the door. "I think I need to have a chat with Miss Foote."

Ginger called out, "Wait!" How she wished she

could go with Basil, but alas, she must remain in her bed for the sake of the baby.

"Yes, Ginger?" Basil said, pausing.

"Take Felicia with you."

Felicia stared at Ginger, then jumped to her feet.

Basil's brow crumpled. "No offence to Felicia, but why would I do that?"

"For the same reason you've grown accustomed to letting me join you. A female presence puts the interviewee at ease. Besides, Felicia was only just there for tea. Miss Foote might consider her a friend and be more willing to expose her secrets."

Basil scrubbed out the wrinkle in his forehead as he sighed. "Very well, then. But—" He gave Felicia a pointed look. "I do *all* the talking. Do you understand?"

Felicia smiled. "Yes, sir." To Ginger, she whispered, "I'll be back straightaway to report on the interview."

Ginger patted Boss' smooth black-and-white head. "I suppose you and I shall wait in the bed. If you like, I'll read to you. The mystery is quite riveting."

he next morning, Ginger was surprised by Pippins' announcement. "You have a visitor, Mrs. Reed. Miss Patricia Foote is waiting in the entrance hall and is quite eager to speak to you. She says it's urgent."

Ginger was all astonishment. Basil and Felicia had recounted their interview with Miss Foote from the night before, and she had been anything but cooperative. In fact, she'd dared Basil to arrest her and, if not, then to leave. She'd refused to discuss the status of her relationship with Mr. Entwistle or Mr. Rothwell. Her arms had folded, and lips had sealed.

"I suppose she'll have to enjoy the pleasure of my company in my room," Ginger said. "Do show her up."

In the habit now of keeping a brush and hand mirror on her bedside table, Ginger brushed her red, bobbed hair and added a bit of lipstick to her naturally pale lips. In anticipation of her guest, she slipped into a fetching little bed jacket made of pink silk, trimmed with white lace, and tied the satin ribbon at her neck into a delicate bow. She then fluffed her pillows, smoothed out her quilt, and got comfortable. Boss, who'd taken to staying at her side rather than Scout's through these last days of her pregnancy, watched from his spot curled up on the bed, with round brown eyes and a questioning tilt of his head.

"One can never be too prepared," she said to him.

Pippins announced Miss Foote, and the woman strolled in like she owned the place. She took a moment to scan the room, her eyes assessing and flashing briefly with approval.

"Good morning, Miss Foote," Ginger said brightly. "To what do I owe the pleasure?"

Standing at the foot of Ginger's bed, Miss Foote clasped her gloved hands. "Your reputation as a lady sleuth precedes you, Mrs. Reed. I'd like to engage Lady Gold Investigations to clear my name. I'm certain you've heard all about certain allegations."

Ginger waved to an empty armchair. "Please have a seat, Miss Foote."

Patricia Foote accepted the offer, placing her small handbag on her lap and crossing her legs at the ankles.

"Now," Ginger started, "I have to confess to feeling

a little bewildered by your request. Certainly, you can see the conflict of interest I would have, should I accept your request. My husband is a chief inspector at Scotland Yard, and then there is our proximity."

"That is precisely why I believe you are the best person for the task. With Chief Inspector Reed in your pocket, as it were, you have access to more inside information than another private investigator might. Better the devil you know, as they say."

Ginger knitted her brows. "It's highly irregular for one to desire to hire a lady in my condition. Are you not fearful that I couldn't do what I must to help you from my position in this room?"

"I believe you to be the type to rely on your brains rather than your mobility, Mrs. Reed. I've been told that Lady Davenport-Witt has been known to work alongside you. She would suffice, would she not, if necessary?"

"Indeed, she would," Ginger said. And she didn't doubt that Felicia would be ecstatic at the prospect. Still, Ginger didn't share Miss Foote's confidence in her own abilities. She'd never solved a crime while being tethered to one spot. However, the challenge *was* tantalising.

Could she do it?

"Before I accept or decline," Ginger said, "would you be prepared to tell me exactly what happened on the day of your grandfather's death, from when you awoke in the morning to the moment you fell asleep that night?"

Miss Foote narrowed her eyes. "Won't that put me in a vulnerable position if you decline?"

"Possibly. But if you want me to prove your innocence, then you're going to have to trust me. And I need to hear your story to determine if I can succeed in achieving your objective."

Miss Foote sighed. "Very well. I've got nothing to hide."

"Before you begin, might I ask why you refused to answer Chief Inspector Reed's questions?"

"Because I was shocked by the implications. I needed time to think things over. I did, and now I'm here." Miss Foote folded her arms. "Shall I begin?"

"Please do."

"The day my grandfather died began no differently from any other day. I awoke naturally sometime after dawn, entered the kitchen around seven and requested a small breakfast of eggs on toast and a cup of tea. Mrs. Garner can vouch for me. Mr. Humphrey brought the paper to the breakfast room. We have it delivered each morning—" she caught Ginger's eye, "much like I assume happens here—"

Ginger nodded. "We subscribe to numerous papers."

"Yes, well, I read *The Telegraph*." She smiled. "After our time in Canada, especially the last few months, it's a relief to read something that isn't mentioning a member of our family."

Except Patricia Foote *had* been mentioned, if not in headline news. Ginger left that nugget for now. She said, "Besides your cook and butler, did anyone else join you for breakfast?"

"My sister, Charlotte. She's always been an early riser. I read her the society pages."

Ginger thought it odd that Patricia Foote would need to read to a girl of thirteen, and Miss Foote read her mind.

"Charlotte is having trouble with her eyes, which explains the headaches she's been having. We've ordered spectacles and expect them to arrive any day." Miss Foote smirked. "She's adamant that she won't wear them, but I suspect practicality will quickly outweigh vanity."

Ginger smiled. "She's a lovely girl, I'm told."

Miss Foote's smile faltered. "Yes. She's had some trouble adjusting."

Ginger commiserated. "All children at that age do. My son, Scout, is entering that awkward age as well. Please do go on."

"I finished breakfast, returned to my room, and bathed and dressed for the day."

"Did you receive any visitors?"

Miss Foote's lips twitched. "I suppose that's the downfall of living in a cul-de-sac. Everyone knows everyone else's business. I'm assuming you're referring to Mr. Entwistle."

"The driver of the green Morgan?"

"Yes. He's a friend."

Ginger arched a brow. "Of the family?"

Miss Foote laughed. "Hardly. Something tells me, Mrs. Reed, that you already know about my personal affairs. Mr. Entwistle and I are engaged."

"I saw the announcement in the newspaper."

"Well, yes. In retrospect, it wasn't a good way to let my family know. You see, my father and grandfather weren't fond of my choice. A notice in the paper was the coward's way out. I see that now."

"Why did they not approve of your choice of marriage partner?"

"Because Murray happens to be related to my late grandmother, God rest her soul. He and I are second cousins, hardly scandalous. So I don't know why they're acting like such crosspatches." Miss Foote's gaze locked on to Ginger. "My grandfather forbade it. My parents, well, they were so weak when it came to him. Even as a slow-moving old man, he had a hold on them. Father actually called the police on Murray and accused him of breaking in!"

"On what evidence?"

A blush blossomed on Miss Foote's cheeks. "A broken garden lattice under my bedroom window. I won't defend him, Mrs. Reed. We are in love, and I told Father as much. I threatened to claw his eyes out on my way to elope if he didn't call off the hounds!"

Oh mercy. Ginger found Miss Foote's angry outburst alarming. Boss roused at the shrill in Miss Foote's voice and crawled to Ginger's side. She scratched his ears to calm him.

"You've recently returned from Canada," Ginger started, "might I ask how your relationship with Mr. Entwistle progressed so quickly?"

"We became reacquainted at a family gathering before our move overseas. There was an immediate attraction, you could say, even at a young age—I was barely older than Charlotte is now—and we decided to become pen pals." Her eyes twinkled at the telling. "We wrote to each other religiously, and eventually fell madly in love."

"What a delightful love story," Ginger said. Pausing briefly, she added, "And what will you do now?"

Miss Foote pouted. "Now I must continue waiting, mustn't I? It would never do to make wedding plans until an acceptable amount of time allotted for mourning has passed."

"Tell me about the argument you had with your grandfather."

Miss Foote's eyes rounded in shock. "Mrs. Reed, you amaze me! Is all of London whispering in your ear?"

Ginger simply smiled. "Miss Foote?"

"Very well. I made another plea for grandfather to reconsider his position regarding Murray, which was useless, once again. Father's threat was just hot air, but Grandfather could truly harm us, so I persisted. How could my marrying Murray affect anyone but me? But grandfather insisted that Murray didn't love me, that he was only trying to weasel into the family to get his hands on grandfather's money."

"Because your grandfather's wealth came from his marriage to Mr. Entwistle's great aunt?" Ginger asked.

"Yes. Grandfather couldn't see past that. The robber was afraid of being robbed in return."

"Does Mr. Entwistle believe his family was robbed?" Ginger asked.

Miss Foote scoffed. "His family *was* robbed. When grandmother passed away, grandfather was supposed to split her wealth between himself and my great-aunts. The greedy old sod refused to do it in the end. So, yes, I admit that Murray's union with me would right some wrongs, but that doesn't mean he doesn't love me too. I can tell whether a man is insincere or not, Mrs. Reed."

"What exactly could your grandfather have done to prevent your marriage to Mr. Entwistle, had he lived?" Ginger asked.

"He was going to cut off my allowance until I broke the engagement. And if I insisted on going through with the wedding, he'd revise the will so I'd never see a penny. He'd prevent my own father from giving me an allowance, just so that Murray and his family could never touch the money."

Ginger let out a long breath. "You must hear how this sounds, Miss Foote. The police will look for motive, opportunity, and means. You have all three. And Mr. Entwistle has at least one. They might try to pin the murder on the two of you if they can find a way to do it."

"That's why I need you." Miss Foote's naturally haughty nature melted away, and suddenly, she appeared to be the very young lady that she was. "I need you to prove my innocence, and Murray's too. We didn't kill my grandfather, Mrs. Reed." She placed a hand on her heart. "I swear."

15

*F*elicia had taken to visiting Hartigan House as part of her new daily routine, so Ginger wasn't surprised to see her when she called.

"I'm not bothering you too much?" Felicia asked as she positioned herself by the window. "I confess that life is just more entertaining around here. There's you, of course, but also Grandmama and Scout." She turned to Ginger. "I didn't realise how much I'd miss everyone. I even miss Pippins, Lizzie, and Mrs. Beasley."

She fell into one of the chairs. "Oh, Ginger, I fear I'll never properly grow into being what society expects of the wife of an earl."

Ginger took Felicia's hand and squeezed. "You mustn't worry about what society thinks. Over time, you will gradually grow into your new status. And I love having you here. We all do. Now, enough of feeling sorry for ourselves."

Felicia straightened her shoulders. "You are right, naturally. Your baby will come, and I'll get the sitting room at Witt House redecorated, and all will be as it should be."

Ginger noted the hint of melancholy in Felicia's voice as she mentioned Witt House and knew she had just the news with which to cheer her former sister-in-law.

"Miss Foote has been to see me this morning," she said.

"Oh?" Felicia's dark brows jumped. "That is rather surprising. The way she treated Basil and me, I thought darkening the door of Hartigan House would be the furthest thing from her mind."

"Yes, well, she changed it after concluding that she and Mr. Entwistle are in real danger of being arrested for murder."

"What did she want from you?"

"She asked to hire me to prove her innocence."

Felicia's eyes widened in surprise. "In your condition?"

"Unlike you, she apparently appreciates that the majority of the work solving a case happens here." Ginger pointed at her temples. "As our Mrs. Christie's Hercule Poirot likes to say, 'with the little grey cells'."

"I do appreciate the use of your little grey cells, Ginger. It's just, well, you're not the creative whim of some mystery-writing author."

"True, but I have you to be my eyes and ears, do I not?"

"Did you take the case?"

"I did, on the provision you'd agree to help me."

Felicia jumped to her feet, spun on her heel to stare at the Foote residence out of the window, then turned to Ginger. She rubbed her palms together. "How shall we start?"

"There's an easel and a large pad of paper in my study. Would you mind bringing it up here?"

Felicia started for the door.

Ginger called after her. "Don't forget a pencil. There's one in the top drawer of my desk."

Felicia returned with a pencil in hand and Lizzie hauling the easel in behind her. Felicia instructed, "At the foot of Mrs. Reed's bed will do. Thank you."

After setting up the easel, Lizzie asked, "Will there be anything else, my lady? Madam?"

"Perhaps some tea," Ginger said.

Lizzie curtsied. "Yes, madam."

"Shall we wait for tea or get started?" Ginger asked Felicia.

"Let's get started," Felicia said eagerly. "Tell me what to write."

"Very well. Make two columns. Title the one on the left 'suspect' and the one on the right 'motive'."

Felicia did as instructed.

"Add Miss Foote to the suspect column and Mr. Entwistle under her name."

Felicia shot Ginger a look. "I thought these two were our clients?"

"They are, but to prove they're without guilt, we need to see what the police see." Ginger arched a brow. "Assuming they are without guilt."

"What if they aren't?"

"I suppose I'll get to keep the deposit but will forfeit the rest of the payment." Ever since Ginger started Lady Gold Investigations, she'd been donating her profits to the Child Wellness Project she'd started with Reverend Oliver Hill at St. George's Church, which offered regular meals to children who lived on the streets of London, as Scout had at one time. Ginger had plenty of money from her inheritance and with her earnings from Feathers & Flair. She was more than happy that her investigative hobby had become profitable and supported such a good cause.

Ginger recited the motives. "Miss Foote was in danger of losing her allowance and ultimate inheritance due to her engagement to Mr. Entwistle. Mr. Entwistle wouldn't want Mr. Rothwell to prevent his marriage to Miss Foote if his sole intent was to get his hands on what was once his family's money."

Felicia whistled. "I can't imagine anyone having a better motive than these two."

"One never knows how great or how small the straw is that breaks the camel's back. Next up, the daughter of the deceased, Mrs. Foote."

Felicia jotted down Virginia Foote. "Her motive?"

Ginger worked her lips. "I understand that Mr. Rothwell intended to leave his wealth to Archibald Foote, being a stickler about passing things down through the males in the family, even if not related by blood. But perhaps Mrs. Foote had induced him to change his mind and worried he might change it back."

Felicia made a face. "Do you think he'd really give his money to Mr. Foote?"

"In trust for his daughter and granddaughters, likely," Ginger said. "Apparently, he underestimated the female mind."

Ginger's thoughts went to Patricia Foote, a female whose mind was, no doubt, intelligent and cunning. Enough to use Ginger for her own devices? Possibly.

"Archibald Foote," Ginger said. "He may also have been nervous about the terms of the will being changed. We must enquire if Mr. Rothwell had rung up his solicitor recently."

Lizzie tapped on the door before bringing in a tray

of tea. "Mrs. Beasley has made shortbread. It's still warm from the oven."

"It smells heavenly," Ginger said, then laughed. "The baby just kicked. I think he or she is eager for me to try one."

After consuming a couple of delicious biscuits, Felicia poured the tea and returned to the drawing board. "Where were we?"

"We mustn't fail to consider the staff," Ginger said. "Miss Foote would like us to remove suspicion of guilt from her and Mr. Entwistle, but I doubt she wishes either of her parents to be found to blame."

"The cook, Mrs. Garner, is new to the Foote household," Felicia said, "so unless there is a past between her and Mr. Rothwell, I can't see her being a suitable suspect."

"I agree, but we must do a little background search," Ginger said. "I'll ask Basil about her, along with the maid, Abby. Write her name down, and Charlotte's too, just in the name of efficiency."

Felicia scribbled on the board. "The other maids are temporary and come and go as the service sends them."

"The man Humphrey works as the family butler," Ginger said, "and also worked as Mr. Rothwell's valet."

"Valets often become confidants over time, but why would he kill his employer?" Felicia placed a hand on a thin hip. "Oh, yes. Miss Foote did mention to me when I called on her that Mr. Rothwell had threatened to give everything to Humphrey to spite them all."

"That would relieve him of motive," Ginger said, "wouldn't it? Unless he was in need of collecting. We should look into his finances." She made another mental note for Basil.

"What if Mr. Rothwell had changed his will in Humphrey's favour and was about to change it back again?"

"So much leans on learning what was in the will and if the solicitor had been rung," Ginger said. "Based on the new evidence of late, Basil has ordered an inquest. Will you be available to attend it with him?"

Felicia grinned. "Of course."

elicia carefully chose an outfit to wear to the inquest. She was there as Ginger's representative, working for their client, Miss Patricia Foote. Yes, a wool suit would be appropriate. Fashionable, like Ginger, yet possessing a sophistication that demanded respect.

Charles entered their bedroom as she modelled the outfit in front of the wooden-framed, full-length mirror precisely angled for her to catch her reflection from head to toe. He stepped in behind her, wrapped his arms around her waist, and snuggled his nose against her neck.

"Beautiful." Then, turning her around, he added, "I still don't understand why you're going to this inquest."

"Of course you do, darling," Felicia said. "I'm

working for Ginger, and she needs me to go in her stead, as she's obviously unable to go herself."

"I'm flabbergasted that she agreed to take on a client in her condition. And a murder case?" Charles stepped closer. "It might become dangerous for you, my love. Why can't you leave it to Basil? Let's you and I do something grand today. Perhaps a trip to Harrods?"

Felicia cocked her head. "Darling, I've been available to you all week, and now, today, at this time, you're free to go shopping?"

"Terrible timing, I admit. I can't help the schedule of the House of Commons."

"The inquest will only take a couple of hours, likely less. Let's plan for luncheon?"

Charles let out a breath of resignation. "Very well. I suppose I can get some work done. I've a pile of papers on my desk in my study."

After kissing Charles goodbye, Felicia took a taxicab to the Old Bailey, an old limestone courthouse in the City of London, where the inquest regarding the death of Crispin Rothwell was being held. Basil had kindly held a seat for her, and she settled in beside him.

He raised a brow. "You made it."

"Why?" Felicia asked. "Am I late?"

Just then, the coroner called the inquest to order, and the doors of the room were closed. Perhaps she had cut it close, but she was here and ready to listen. She cast a glance about the room. With a becoming netted brim, her angled hat provided a shield from which she could view a person without being caught staring. Clad in black, the whole Foote clan was there, including the young Miss Charlotte, who, from Felicia's position across the room, seemed to stare blankly. Poor girl, having experienced the trauma of finding her grandfather waxy and not breathing. The only other person Felicia recognised was Dr. Longden, his expression long and dark, aggravated, likely by his new, yet ill-fitting, spectacles which kept slipping down his nose.

"Please, everyone," the coroner started, "come to order."

The room fell into a hush.

"Today, we are here to establish the identity of the deceased, the place and time of death, and to determine how the deceased came by his death." A slight murmuring broke the silence. "Would Mr. Archibald Foote come to the stand?"

Mr. Foote, caught playing nervously with his long moustache, rose to his feet. Once he'd taken his position behind the podium, and sworn an oath to tell the truth, the coroner instructed an officer to show him the photographs.

"Can you confirm the identity of the deceased?" the coroner asked.

Mr. Foote was provided with a photograph.

Mr. Foote cleared his throat. "That is my father-in-law, Mr. Crispin Rothwell."

The coroner continued, "From your perspective, please relay how the day of Mr. Rothwell's death unfolded."

"Yes, well . . ." Mr. Foote fussed with his tie. "It was a day like any other. After breakfast, we all went about our business. My father-in-law had breakfast brought to his room on a tray."

"Was that typical of Mr. Rothwell?" the coroner asked.

"Well, yes. At least lately. Especially since our return from Canada. The journey was rather arduous and took a lot out of the old gentleman, I'm afraid."

"Did you go to see him that morning?" the coroner asked.

"I did."

"Was that typical?"

"Well, not so typical. But I had a question for him."

"And that was?"

"Well, nothing of consequence. I can't rightly remember."

The coroner scowled. "Do try, Mr. Foote."

"Right, yes, well, er, if I recall, I meant to ask my father-in-law about my daughter Patricia."

"What about her?"

"Well, er, it's rather delicate."

"If you refuse to reveal it here, Mr. Foote, I assure you, it will come out in the courts."

"Yes, right, very well." Mr. Foote cast a disconcerted glance toward his family. Mrs. Foote and Miss Foote sat still and wide-eyed. Miss Charlotte seemed lost in her own world.

Mr. Foote continued. "I only wanted to reason with my father-in-law regarding his stubborn refusal to consider Patricia's betrothed, Mr. Murray Entwistle."

"I see," the coroner said. "Is Mr. Entwistle in the room?"

"No, he's not."

"Am I to surmise that Mr. Rothwell was not in favour of a union between Mr. Entwistle and Miss Patricia Foote?"

"That's correct."

"Did he give a reason why?"

Mr. Foote blanched, then, Felicia was quite certain, lied. "No. I believe in his befuddled mind that no young man would've suited him. This was the topic of concern of the day. Each member of the family, in turn, tried to convince him to see reason."

"And did he?" the coroner asked.

"No, sir. We'd tired ourselves out and decided to leave the matter for another day."

"Can you explain the charred cushion with the blood on it?"

Mr. Foote hesitated before answering. "Only that my father-in-law must've grabbed it when in need then left it on the floor. One of the maids must've considered it too spoiled to repair and thrown it in the fire."

The coroner, seemingly satisfied by Mr. Foote's accounting, excused Mrs. Foote and both Miss Footes from giving evidence.

Felicia stared at Basil, whose hazel eyes were narrowed, his lips working as he considered what he'd heard. Had he caught Mr. Foote's lie? *Had the man actually lied?* Felicia was no longer certain. Everything he said made perfect sense and lined up with what she'd heard from Mrs. Schofield. Though, hadn't Mr. Foote called the police on Mr. Entwistle? Clearly, he wasn't in favour of the union himself. And from what the other family members had said about Mr. Rothwell, he was stubborn and belligerent but not befuddled. He most definitely disliked Mr. Entwistle particularly.

"I'd like to call Dr. Longden," the coroner said.

Dr. Longden pushed up on his spectacles as he headed for the stand. Felicia had known the doctor for a few years, and he always seemed old to her, but for some reason, he appeared to have aged even more. His new spectacles didn't help. They magnified his eyes and the wrinkled skin around them.

"Dr. Longden, please relay the events of the day Mr. Rothwell lost his life, to the best of your recollection."

Dr. Longden's gaze remained cast downward, which resulted in the slippage of his spectacles. With a long finger, he pushed them along the bridge of his nose.

"Well, on that morning, I was called to see a patient who lives across the road from the deceased. I saw her and then returned to my surgery. A short while later, I received an urgent call to come to the new residence of the Foote family."

"Was Mr. Rothwell a regular patient of yours?" the coroner asked.

"No, but I've seen to his daughter, Mrs. Virginia Foote, and her daughters over the years." Dr. Longden cast a glance at the Foote family. "It was Mrs. Foote who rang me."

The coroner studied his notes then asked, "You arrived at the Foote residence at what time?"

"I checked my pocket watch when I arrived. It was ten past one."

The coroner nodded, and Dr. Longden continued. "I knocked on the door and was let in by the family butler, Humphrey, who escorted me upstairs to the bedroom of the deceased."

"He was already dead?"

Dr. Longden stared at the coroner. "He was already dead. Of course, I tried to revive him."

"At any point in your examination, did you see evidence of foul play?"

"Not at first glance. For a man in his condition—elderly, frail, and excuse me for saying this, but of a difficult temperament that can cause heart strain—it appeared that he'd suffered a heart attack or stroke."

"Which was it, doctor? A heart attack or stroke?"

"A heart attack."

"I understand blood was found on the nose of the deceased," the coroner said.

"It's not uncommon for physical stress to bring on a nosebleed," Dr. Longden returned.

"And what of the bloodied cushion that was found in the fireplace?"

"Nothing has been determined as yet. There are a variety of possible explanations."

"Thank you, Dr. Longden," the coroner said. "You may return to your seat. Would Mr. Bertram Atkinson please take the stand."

Felicia glanced at Basil, and he mouthed, "Rothwell's solicitor."

Mr. Atkinson was a short man with a slight belly

bulge and a halo of grey on a round bald head. He wore an ill-fitting suit and a grim expression.

"Mr. Atkinson," the coroner said. "It's come to my attention that you'd been to visit Mr. Rothwell in the early morning hours on the day of his death."

Felicia regarded Basil with surprise. By the way Basil wrinkled his nose, it was apparent that he hadn't been made aware of such a visit, either.

"Yes, sir," Mr. Atkinson said. "He arranged for me to come early so as not to rouse the suspicion of his family members." He pointedly did not look in the direction of the Foote family whose faces had soured further, if that were possible.

"And what was it that Mr. Rothwell wanted?"

A murmur arose from the attendees at the coroner's personal question.

Mr. Atkinson sniffed. "I'm still bound by client privilege."

"I'm attempting to determine if there are grounds for motive for murder, Mr. Atkinson," the coroner said. "Without revealing details of the client's legal needs, can you tell this court if you believe your visit would have resulted in the provision of motive to injure your client? To clarify, was a changing of the will involved?"

"To answer both questions, yes."

The room erupted in exclamations of shock and protestation.

Mr. Foote jumped to his feet. "That's outrageous!"

"Order!" the coroner demanded. "Order!"

After a loud bang of the gavel on its block, the grumbling subsided. The coroner wrapped up the session by saying, "Mr. Crispin Rothwell's death remains suspicious, and continued investigation into the matter is required."

Felicia, along with everyone else in the room, stared at the Foote family. Patricia Foote caught her eye and stared with a look that dared Felicia to fail. Miss Foote was counting on Felicia and Ginger to prove her innocence more than ever.

The problem was, Felicia was certain Mr. Rothwell's granddaughter was guilty of something, and quite possibly, it was murder.

inger heard Basil and Felicia entering Hartigan House and could barely wait until they got upstairs. She spoke before they had both made it inside her bedroom. "I do want to hear how it went," Ginger said, "but my body craves a hot soaking, and Lizzie is now drawing my bath. Can you give me a summary with the details to follow later?"

"The coroner declared it suspicious and worth continued investigation," Basil said.

"Oh mercy," Ginger replied. She turned to Felicia. "And how did our client take it?"

"We didn't speak, but if her look could have set the coroner's bench on fire, the whole building would be in flames right now." Felicia pushed up her sleeves. "Why don't I assist in Lizzie's place and recite it all while you soak in bath salts."

Ginger smiled. "That sounds marvellous."

"I have to get back to the Yard," Basil said. "I've no time to waste now that this is an official murder case." He kissed Ginger on the head. "Besides, I don't think you can get into too much trouble in the bath. I'll see you at dinner."

The bathroom was a new addition, taking a small room at the end of the corridor. On black-and-white tiles, a claw-foot bathtub was filled with water that Lizzie had drawn and smelled of lavender. A modern flush toilet had been installed in the corner, and a sink was crowned with a large mirror.

Ginger dropped her robe to the floor, and Felicia offered her arm, ensuring a safe entry into the bathtub.

"Thank you, love," Ginger said.

Felicia sat on the padded velvet stool. "I'll be quick and finish before the water cools."

"Grand idea."

Felicia recounted the details, including what everyone was wearing and highlights of the intriguing parts.

"Mr. Foote thinks his father-in-law grabbed the small cushion to stay the blood flow, and it fell to the floor when he had finished with it. In all the frantic comings and goings when Mr. Rothwell was found dead, apparently no one noticed the cushion. He's presuming one of the maids must have considered the damage too dire and threw it in the fire instead of trying to clean it."

Ginger ducked under the water to wet her hair, then, after wiping water from her face, said, "Which one threw it into the fire? Not Abby, by her own accounting."

"No one seems to know." Felicia dropped a bit of soap into her palm then worked it into Ginger's hair. Ginger enjoyed the light massage, but more than that, she was delighted at how this case was bringing her and Felicia together.

Ginger indicated that she was ready to get out, and Felicia scooped up the towel and extended her arm. After the sloshing of the water had subsided, Felicia continued, "Mr. Rothwell's solicitor, Mr. Atkinson, made a stir."

Ginger held the towel, which barely fit around her swollen body, as Felicia helped her into her house-coat, then let the towel fall to the floor. "Please, do tell."

"On the day Mr. Rothwell died, Mr. Atkinson had visited in the early morning, allegedly to make adjust-ments to his will. The coroner concluded it was enough to suggest that someone in the family had motive."

Ginger used a small comb to part her bobbed, red locks to one side and pushed the tips behind her ears.

"I can see why Miss Patricia Foote would be none too happy about that."

"The whole family was staring daggers," Felicia said. "And I can't say I blame them."

Once Ginger, with Felicia's assistance, was settled in bed, she said, "Perhaps you could drop in at the Foote residence and speak to the maids. It would be helpful to know who attempted to destroy that cushion."

"Wouldn't it appear odd for me to be nosing about at the back entrance in search of the maids?" Felicia asked.

"Take Lizzie with you. She'll help make the other maids feel more at ease. Go on the pretence of neighbourly concern."

"Very well. I may make a fool of myself, but it's for a good cause."

"Indeed," Ginger said with a smile. "Finding a murderer is always a good cause."

18

Felicia liked to think of herself as a person who didn't consider herself above another, despite Britain's entrenched class system. Yet, she couldn't deny feeling uncomfortable walking to the back entrance of the Foote residence like a servant. She caught herself casting a glance over her shoulder to ensure she wasn't spotted. The cul-de-sac was hardly a busy thoroughfare. Still, she was Lady Davenport-Witt, and should an unscrupulous citizen see her behaving like a servant, it could cause a minor scandal in the society section of the London rags. The cool weather allowed for a muffler and propped-up collar of her jacket, which helped conceal her face.

Lizzie walked dutifully behind her, which was silly since she was the one who knew the way. The path was straightforward enough, and after reminding herself of the important nature of her call, Felicia put her shoulders back and marched on.

"Shall I do the knocking, Miss Gol—my lady?" Lizzie asked.

"Please do," Felicia replied. She stepped into a gazebo—once hidden in vines, but now more exposed with the dropping of the autumn leaves—in the back garden, to an agreed-upon meeting place and awaited the first maid to appear. It was up to Lizzie to get them to come to her.

Through the thinning vines, Felicia saw Lizzie disappear into the kitchen. After a few minutes, Felicia was glad she'd worn her muffler, not only to help to hide her identity but now for the warmth it provided.

Eventually, the kitchen door opened, and a maid with a pinched face scampered to the gazebo. Felicia stood.

"Please be at ease. I thank you for coming to speak to me. I'm Lady Davenport-Witt. What is your name?"

The maid curtsied. "I'm Chrissy, my lady."

"I've only a few questions for you, Chrissy. Can I count on you to be discreet?"

"Yes, my lady." Chrissy's eyes darted to the kitchen door, and Felicia knew she needed to be quick before the maid's absence was noted.

"It's about the cushion that was found in Mr. Roth-well's fireplace. It's my understanding that the cushion was a personal item belonging to Mr. Rothwell. I'm only interested in knowing who threw it into the fireplace. There will be no repercussions for the action, so you may speak freely. Did you throw it out, Chrissy?"

"No, my lady. I would tell you if I did, but I didn't, I swear. It wasn't me. I'm a parlour maid. I never go upstairs."

Felicia found she believed the nervous maid. "Do you know who did?"

With a firm shake of the head, Chrissy answered, "No, my lady."

"Who was cleaning the bedrooms that day?"

"Abby Green, my lady."

"And no one else?"

"Mary Ann worked in the morning, but it was her half-day." She cast another glance at the kitchen door.

"Thank you, Chrissy. You may go."

Chrissy bobbed then darted back to the house.

Mary Ann, in contrast to the younger Chrissy, was tall and stern-faced. Clearly, she'd worked amongst the gentry for a long time and no longer held them in esteem and barely cloaked her disdain. She bent stiffly at the knees. "My lady. You wish to speak to me?"

"Yes. I realise this is slightly unorthodox, but I hope to have your cooperation."

"Of course, my lady."

"And your discretion."

"Of course, my lady."

"I understand you worked upstairs the morning of Mr. Rothwell's death."

"Yes, my lady."

"Did you see Mr. Rothwell?"

"Yes, my lady. He preferred my assistance as I've been with the family for many years, excepting the years they were in Canada. I bring him his breakfast along with the morning paper."

Felicia asked Mary Ann the same questions about the bloodied cushion.

"I know the cushion well, my lady. It was a gift from his late wife and personally monogrammed by her."

"It had sentimental value?"

Mary Ann blinked. "I wouldn't call Mr. Rothwell sentimental, but yes, he had an attachment to the small cushion."

"Did you throw the cushion into the fire, Mary Ann?"

The maid looked offended. "I certainly did not, my lady. Knowing how Mr. Rothwell felt about it, I would've done my best to have it cleaned. It was only blood, and one can clean blood from garments if one knows what one is doing."

Felicia was quite certain the maid Mary Ann was "one who knew".

The parade of family members had happened late morning, and as far as Felicia knew, it was only Mary Ann who'd seen Mr. Rothwell before then. "Did anyone else see Mr. Rothwell that morning?"

Mary Ann sniffed. "Humphrey, my lady."

As the butler or valet? "Was it customary for Humphrey to see Mr. Rothwell at this time?"

"He helped Mr. Rothwell dress for the day, after he finished breakfast, only—"

"Yes?" Felicia prompted.

"Well, he came up earlier than usual. I passed him on the stairs, and we normally don't see each other. Our duties require us to go upstairs at different times."

Felicia got the distinct impression that Mary Ann didn't care for Humphrey. "Do you know why Humphrey went up early that day?"

"No, my lady, and he wouldn't tell the likes of me. All I can say is that Mr. Rothwell had asked me to tell Humphrey that he wouldn't require assistance. I believe he was upset by something he read in the papers."

Felicia doubted Mary Ann's supposed naiveté. The engagement would've been all the talk going on below stairs.

"Did you tell Humphrey this?"

Mary Ann nodded. "Yes, my lady. He went up

anyway, and when I persisted, he told me to mind my own business."

After dismissing Mary Ann, Felicia headed back towards Hartigan House—Lizzie had returned—but just as she reached the wrought-iron gate, she spun on her heels and strolled across the court to the front door of the Foote residence and rang the bell.

As expected, the door was answered by the squirrelly-looking butler.

"Good afternoon, Humphrey," Felicia said, putting on a smile.

He bowed slightly. "I'm afraid Miss Foote is indisposed."

"It would please me if you'd give me a few moments of your time."

Humphrey couldn't have looked more startled than if Felicia had just asked him to dance in the street. He gathered his senses quickly, stepped outside, and closed the door.

"My lady," he said, his voice pitching higher with nerves. "How can I help you?"

"You may not be aware, but Mrs. Reed is a respected private investigator, and I often work as her assistant. A member of the Foote family has retained us to assist with this unfortunate circumstance which has brought on the attention of the police. Can I count on your cooperation and discretion?"

With a slight nod of his head, Humphrey said, "Of course, my lady."

"I understand you were with Mr. Rothwell the morning he passed away."

"Indeed, I was, my lady. It was customary for me to help Mr. Rothwell dress after he had finished his breakfast."

"So, it was a morning like any other morning?"

"Yes, my lady."

"You didn't alter the time in any way, perhaps arriving to assist Mr. Rothwell earlier than usual?"

Humphrey sniffed. "I suppose I might've gone earlier. I wasn't watching the time."

"You weren't?" Felicia exaggerated a look of shock. "I would think a member of staff of your stature, acting both as the family butler and Mr. Rothwell's valet, would be very keenly aware of the time."

Humphrey's cheeks blossomed a deep red. "I assure you, my lady, that I attend to my duties in an orderly manner."

"It was revealed at the inquest that Mr. Rothwell's solicitor visited early that morning."

"He did, my lady. I let him inside myself, but I didn't go into Mr. Rothwell's room at his request. Mr. Atkinson has been before and knew the way."

"It's my understanding that Mr. Rothwell had also

requested that you *not* come to him after breakfast as usual, but you went anyway."

Stiffening, Humphrey said, "I will assume that you spoke to Mary Ann. All I will say about that is you must take whatever she says with a pinch of salt. As to Mr. Rothwell, I couldn't count on a maid's word and needed to ensure for myself that I was unneeded."

"Was Mr. Rothwell upset about something?"

"Lady Davenport-Witt, I have been most accommodating—"

"I can assure you that the police questioning will be more demanding," Felicia said, then softened her tone. "I'm on the side of the family. I'm here to help."

"Mr. Rothwell had read something distasteful in the papers—"

"The engagement announcement of Miss Patricia Foote and Mr. Entwistle?"

"Yes. Mr. Rothwell was very displeased. Now, my lady, if you'll excuse me, I'm needed inside. Mr. Foote is sorting through Mr. Rothwell's things. He's taken me on as his valet," Humphrey said with a note of importance. "I'm grateful to be retained, but it will take time for both of us to get used to each other."

"Of course," Felicia said. "Thank you, Humphrey."

As Felicia returned to Hartigan House and up the staircase to Ginger's room, she felt more confused about the case than ever.

inger hated to complain. Compared with many people, she had it very good: love, friendships, social respect, two successful businesses, and the comfort and status that wealth brings. But blast it, how her back hurt! And her bones felt loose at the joints as if they'd lost connective tissue. Matilda had reassured her that was normal, just her body getting ready to perform a miracle.

No matter how Ginger positioned herself on the bed, new aches and pains presented themselves. The baby moved about, putting pressure on her bladder, kidneys, and stomach, and often gave her ribs a good kicking. The child would be spirited, that was for certain. Ginger rubbed her belly, thinking there just wasn't enough room for everything going on in there.

Remaining in bed wasn't what was called for, was it? Ginger wanted the baby out!

She sighed as she once again plumped her pillows and resigned herself to her fate. She wasn't about to defy the doctor's orders. She'd sacrifice anything for the health and well-being of this child, including endless trips to the loo and painful indigestion.

Ginger picked up her book, entertained by the plight of Hercule Poirot, but her mind kept returning to the case on her own street. She checked her watch. Where was Felicia, anyway? Certainly, she'd have finished speaking to the Foote family maids by now.

Nibbling on another biscuit from the tray Lizzie had left her that morning, Ginger feared she'd have more than just baby weight to lose when all was said and done. At this point, one more wouldn't hurt. She sipped her tea and plucked another biscuit from the tray.

Just as she'd turned the page to end a chapter, she heard Felicia's voice in the corridor. "Is Mrs. Reed available?"

"Yes, madam," came a maid's voice. "Her door is open."

Felicia blew in, and Ginger put her book aside. "Felicia, you're flushed," Ginger said. "You must have news."

Felicia removed her muffler. "I'm flushed because

I've just come in from the cold and skipped up the staircase, but yes, I do have news, I think."

"Join me for tea," Ginger said. "The pot is still hot, and the biscuits are divine."

"I will," Felicia said as she removed her coat and gloves, leaving them on the foot of Ginger's bed. She poured herself a cup of tea and bit into a biscuit. "Investigative work stirs the appetite."

"Indeed," Ginger said. "Now, tell me everything."

"The young maid, Chrissy, a nervous sort, didn't have much to contribute except to say that Abby hadn't been the only maid to work on the upper floor that morning. Mary Ann, who has been with the family for some time, had also worked there but had the afternoon off and wasn't at the house when all the commotion transpired."

"Did you get a chance to speak to her?"

"Yes. She was very close-lipped, well trained in that regard, but I did manage to get her to open up a little at the end of our short conversation. I can tell you that there's no love lost between her and Humphrey. I sensed a little rivalry going on between the two." Felicia pressed a finger against her cheek. "It was Mary Ann's job to take a breakfast tray to Mr. Rothwell, along with the morning paper."

"She was with him when he read the news about his granddaughter's engagement?"

"Yes, and according to her, he didn't take the news well."

"What did she say about the cushion?"

"She insisted that she'd never throw it away, blood or no, because it had a special place in Mr. Rothwell's heart."

Ginger raised a brow.

"That's what I thought too," Felicia said. "He was hardly the sentimental type, but apparently it was handsewn by his late wife."

"Perhaps he truly loved her," Ginger said. "Her loss could explain his bristly demeanour, at least in part. If what Mary Ann believes is true, then it's hard to imagine Mr. Rothwell using that particular cushion to stay a nosebleed. There were other pillows and blankets, not to mention his own nightclothes, that he could've opted for. Did Mary Ann say anything else?"

"That Humphrey had also gone to the deceased's room that morning, after her. It was his custom to go up after breakfast to help Mr. Rothwell dress, but the timing was designed so that he and Mary Ann never passed each other on the stairs."

Ginger narrowed her gaze in question. "That morning was different?"

"Mary Ann says he went up to see Mr. Rothwell earlier than usual, even though she'd told him that Mr. Rothwell didn't want to see him at all that day."

"How curious," Ginger said. "Why wouldn't Mr. Rothwell want his valet?"

"Mary Ann said he was too upset about the engagement announcement, but that didn't make sense to me either. So I decided to have a little chat with Humphrey."

Ginger smiled. "That's why it took you so long to come back. Please, do tell!"

"Humphrey didn't appreciate my questioning him," Felicia said, "and would've refused if the protocol had allowed for it. He did an admirable job of answering without saying anything of import, though I believe it's why he was running to see him earlier than their normal schedule."

"Perhaps to intercept the newspaper once he realised what was in its pages? He might've feared the engagement announcement would be upsetting."

"He tried to change the subject by bringing Mr. Foote into the conversation." Felicia smiled crookedly. "A misstep on his part."

"How so?"

"He said Mr. Foote needed him to help him sort through Mr. Rothwell's things."

Ginger huffed. "So soon? The man isn't even buried yet."

Felicia stated triumphantly, "And, he's already taken Humphrey on to act as his valet."

"Interesting," Ginger said. "One could say Mr. Foote was acting a mite impetuously, overly eager to appropriate the role of family patriarch."

"That was my thought too."

"It's motive," Ginger started.

Felicia clapped her hands. "Is Mr. Foote our murderer?"

Ginger loved Felicia's enthusiasm. "You've done a good job with the case so far," she said, "but let's not get ahead of ourselves."

A knock on the door presented Pippins, who looked rather flushed. "Miss Patricia Foote is here to see you, madam. I asked her to wait, but—"

To Ginger's astonishment, Miss Foote pushed past Pippins as she stepped into the room. Her expression was stricken, and Ginger braced herself for bad news. She shared a look with Felicia before asking, "What is the matter, Miss Foote?"

"It's Murray, Mrs. Reed. He's been arrested! You must do something!"

20

Ginger stared back at her uninvited guest, feeling a little shocked that she hadn't first heard the news from Basil. "When did this happen?"

"Only minutes ago." Miss Foote waved the handkerchief she held in one hand. "I received an urgent message from Mr. Atkinson, our solicitor, informing me of this utterly distressing news. He had hopes of sparing me and my reputation, but it's too late for that, isn't it? Our engagement was in the papers the day Grandfather died, and now this!" She collapsed into a chair, pressed her handkerchief to her face, and sobbed.

Ginger looked at Felicia, who lifted her shoulders and stared back with a questioning look.

"Miss Foote," Ginger began, "is there anything more you can tell us? Details of the arrest?"

"Only that Murray couldn't have done it—he was with me early in the afternoon."

"Where exactly were you and Mr. Entwistle during that time?" Felicia asked.

"We took a stroll through Hyde Park."

Ginger inclined her head. "Did anyone see you?"

"It started to rain," Miss Foote said, "and we were concealed under a shared umbrella. The park was nearly vacant, and I'm afraid that no one saw us. But shouldn't it be enough that I was with Murray? Does that not secure an alibi?"

"Had someone seen you, certainly," Ginger said. "But it appears that you may be under suspicion as well."

"I know that already," Miss Foote snapped. "It's why I've engaged you. So why have they arrested Murray?"

"My guess is they suspect collusion between the two of you," Ginger replied. Then to Felicia, she said, "Would you mind escorting Miss Foote back to her home?"

Miss Foote jumped to her feet. "Is that it? Have you finished with me?"

"Not at all, Miss Foote," Ginger said kindly. "Allow me some time to make a few calls and ask questions on your behalf. I'll notify you when I've learned something new."

Ginger nodded at Felicia, who then slipped into her coat and walked out with Miss Foote. Ginger rang the bell for Pippins.

Moments later, he arrived. "Yes, madam?"

"Please ring Scotland Yard for me and ask for Mr. Reed. Tell him I need to speak to him, and I'll walk down the corridor to the library to use the telephone if necessary."

Pippins nodded and disappeared into the corridor. Leaning back on her pillows, Ginger closed her eyes. Her mind worked on the puzzle before her. Clearly, the police had enough evidence against Mr. Entwistle to warrant an arrest. Had he been to see Mr. Rothwell that morning as well? That would be three to see the victim in the morning that Ginger knew of—Mary Ann, Humphrey, and now Mr. Entwistle if this was the case—and all four of the Foote family members after that.

Mr. Entwistle had a motive. Marrying Patricia Foote would give him influence with the family and an opportunity to recover the money procured from his mother's side through his great-aunt's marriage to Mr. Rothwell.

Pippins returned with a message from Basil. "He'll be home for luncheon, madam, and would be pleased to share it with you here, in this room. He was quite precise about that."

Ginger smiled. "Thank you, Pippins."

KNOWING Basil was on his way, Ginger spent the time freshening up, using her permitted journey to the bathroom to wash her face and clean her teeth. She then put on a clean nightgown, brushed her bob until it shone, pinning it off her face with a pearl-encrusted hairpin. She might be nearly nine months pregnant and what felt like twice her normal size, but she still wanted to be attractive in her husband's eyes, something he reassured her constantly she always would be, even with a frock that looked like a potato sack and months of poor sleep.

Feeling confident and eager, Ginger waited in her bed and maybe even dozed off a little. Before she knew it, her eyes fluttered open, and Basil was sitting at her side, regarding her with fondness.

"How are you, love?" he asked.

Ginger shifted to a higher seated position. "I'm well, darling. I've heard you've had an eventful day already."

"Yes, well, let's discuss it over lunch, shall we?" Basil said. "I've already made arrangements with the kitchen for it to be brought up."

"Splendid."

Basil helped Ginger out of bed and to the table by the window.

"My week of bedrest is almost up," Ginger said, her voice tinged with relief. She was more than ready to be on her feet again, free to go where she liked, knowing it would be safe for her baby.

"Not until tomorrow," Basil said. "Dr. Longden is coming to see you in the morning, is he not?"

Ginger relented. "Yes, first thing." She could survive one more day.

Lizzie and Grace arrived, each carrying a tray, one with the food and one with the tea. Soon Ginger and Basil were enjoying cold meat sandwiches and a fruit salad expertly prepared by Mrs. Beasley. Ginger thought the woman a godsend and didn't know what the family would do without her. Perhaps she could recommend a suitable nanny? She hadn't thought about Mrs. Beasley's connection to the service community before.

The weather outside was dreary grey, with dark clouds floating along the skyline. With that backdrop, the Foote residence looked morbidly melancholy.

"I had a visit from Miss Patricia Foote," Ginger started. "She was terribly upset upon hearing about her fiancé's arrest."

"Imaginably so," Basil admitted.

"What evidence did the police find to make such a move?"

"There is a trellis at the back of the house, with evidence that it had been scaled recently," Basil said. "A wooden lattice is broken, and edges of the stone and brick are scuffed as well. Shoe prints in the damp ground match Entwistle's shoes. He admits to climbing it, to be entertained by Miss Foote, clandestinely."

"Young lovers often go to great extents to be together, especially if their union has been forbidden," Ginger said. "Was there damage to the window? Proof of breaking and entering?"

"No. According to Entwistle, Miss Foote purposely left the window unlocked."

"Basil, love, I fail to see the crime here."

"The scaling of the wall and entry into an unmarried lady's bedroom is a misdemeanour."

"Misdemeanour isn't murder."

"No, but it leads to opportunity and means." Basil gave her a look. "And we already know he has motive."

"Do you have any proof, real proof, that Mr. Entwistle was in Mr. Rothwell's room the day that he died?"

Basil shook his head. "No, and this was my argument to Morris. But Rothwell had influence in certain back rooms, and Morris insisted that we 'solve' this case as soon as possible."

Superintendent Morris—arrogant and pompous—had only gained his position at the Yard because of who he knew in parliament, not due to skill and experience. Ginger shook her head. "Even if it means arresting the wrong person?"

"Is he the wrong person, though?" Basil asked. "Do you have an alternative suspect?"

"There are a few who could fit the bill," Ginger said. "But top of the list is Mr. Archibald Foote. Humphrey let it slip to Felicia that Mr. Foote was already clearing out Mr. Rothwell's things, and the man isn't even buried yet. And he's got Humphrey working as his valet too. It seems to me Mr. Foote is overly eager to take on the duties of the patriarch."

"You think he'd kill just to have his father-in-law's rooms and valet?" Basil asked.

"It's been well documented that Mr. Rothwell was a demanding and often unreasonable man," Ginger replied. "Perhaps Mr. Foote had reached his limit of endurance."

"It's possible, I suppose."

"I'm only saying that the evidence against Mr. Entwistle so far wouldn't go very far in a court of law, not when it would be so easy to cast doubt."

Basil reached over and pushed a lock of Ginger's red hair behind her ear. "You're so adorable."

"Adorable? I'm hardly shooting for adorable, Basil."

Basil smiled. "You can't help it, love. Your passion for life and justice just makes you more beautiful." He lifted her hand to his lips and kissed it. "If we weren't already married, I'd ask you right now."

Ginger rarely blushed, but she felt herself doing so in that moment. "Basil, I'm trying to be serious."

"I know." Basil pushed his empty plate aside. "I need to go back to work. I'll present your case to Morris. I suspect he already knows he's standing on one leg. I just need to give him a little shove."

Movement outside caught Ginger's eye. "Is that Dr. Longden?"

Basil swivelled to stare out the window. "I don't see anyone."

"He disappeared to the back of the Foote residence. I'm sure it was him."

Standing, Basil craned his neck to look down the road. "I don't see his motorcar."

Ginger tapped her lips with a finger. "Perhaps I was mistaken. In this weather, all men dress alike."

Basil slipped into his dark-brown overcoat and placed a matching trilby on his head.

Ginger smiled and nodded to him with her chin. "Case in point."

21

*G*inger had been awake for two hours by the time Dr. Longden came to check up on her the next morning. She'd washed, eaten, and dressed in anticipation. Never had she been so eager to see a physician in her life, but today her hopes rested on this man to free her from the confines of her blasted bedroom!

Pippins would've relieved him of his hat and coat—no doubt dripping with the rain that fell incessantly these days, as he entered hatless, his white shirt wrinkled, his tie askew, and carrying his black doctor's bag.

"Good morning, Mrs. Reed," he said. Never an overly cheery fellow, Dr. Longden's spirits reflected the weather outside. Determined to lighten the mood, Ginger smiled and said brightly, "Good morning,

Doctor. So good to see you today. And of course, you know I'm hoping for good news."

"Yes, well, you made it through last week, and every additional week is good for the baby's health."

Dr. Longden removed the stethoscope from his bag, plugged his ears with the ear pieces, and placed the scope in his hand.

"Please do warm that thing up," Ginger said with a chuckle. "Or the startle from the cold metal might just put me into labour."

As instructed, Dr. Longden gave it a good rub before checking her heartbeat, then the baby's. After that, he felt her belly, and Ginger was grateful his hands were warm.

"Everything sounds good," he said. "The baby's in the correct position."

"I'm so excited to meet him or her," Ginger said. "I understand the reasoning for such a long gestation. By the time we ladies get to nine months, we're ready to go through anything to get the baby out into the world."

That brought a smile to the doctor's face, and Ginger felt her mission for the day was accomplished. Because now, she had a few rather uncomfortable questions to ask. "Dr. Longden, on a different note, I wonder if you'd enlighten me?"

The doctor put his stethoscope back into the black bag and closed it. "I'd be happy to, Mrs. Reed."

"It's about Mr. Rothwell."

Dr. Longden stiffened at the mention of the dead man's name. "Yes?"

"There seems to be some confusion as to the cause of death. Was it a heart attack or suffocation? The charred cushion with the bloodstain in evidence is raising the question."

Dr. Longden grimaced, causing his spectacles to slip off the bridge of his nose. With a long finger, he pushed them back.

"A heart attack was a natural conclusion before foul play was suspected. Now, if you don't mind, Mrs. Reed. I have other appointments."

"Of course." She stared at the doctor until she caught his eye and then smiled. "You know my mind. I'm naturally curious." She patted her stomach. "Hopefully, we'll see you soon."

"Not too soon, Mrs. Reed." Dr. Longden looked relieved to be back on the topic of Ginger's impending birth. "You no longer have to stay on bed rest, but I do recommend that you avoid the stairs as much as possible."

Ginger clapped her hands. "Great news, Doctor!"

"Yes. Good day, Mrs. Reed."

Ginger swung her feet to the floor, but before she could stand, the doctor had left.

Boss, his stubby tail wagging, his pink tongue hanging, traipsed in at that moment, and Ginger directed her comment to him. "He's a strange man, boy."

As Ginger slipped her arms into her dressing gown, Boss ran to the window, perhaps catching sight of a winter bird swooping by, and barked. Ginger glanced out in time to see Dr. Longden disappear behind the Foote residence. "It *was* him I saw yesterday."

Ginger stared at the damp and dreary-looking house across the street and murmured, "Was that his next appointment, Bossy?"

Ginger rang the bell, and Lizzie appeared shortly afterwards.

"Yes, madam?" Lizzie asked as she curtsied.

"Dr. Longden has given me the all-clear to get out of bed! I long to change out of this deplorable pyjama top." Ginger had outgrown most of her lovely night-gowns and had taken to wearing Basil's pyjama tops instead. She waved at her wardrobe. "There must be something suitable that I can still fit into."

Lizzie opened the double wooden doors of the wardrobe and fished through the frocks that hung there. As the months had passed, items too small were removed and replaced by larger items Ginger had handpicked from her shop, Feathers & Flair. But there was a limit to how many overly large items Ginger would allow herself to hoard.

"How about this one?" Lizzie held up a layered frock at least three sizes larger than normal.

Not entirely in love with the item, Ginger hummed. She would feel like she was donning an over-priced tent no matter which one she wore. "That would be fine."

Lizzie's help was always appreciated, but especially so in these final days of Ginger's pregnancy, when she found her balance questionable and her ability to touch her toes impossible.

Once dressed, she settled at her dressing table and stared into the mirror.

"Would you like my help with your hair, madam?" Lizzie asked.

Ginger considered her reflection. The nice thing about a trendy bob was that even a person in her condition could brush and style it.

"I can manage, Lizzie," she said. "I'd like to have lunch in the library—" Ginger thought she'd heed Dr. Longden's remarks about the stairs, at least for the day. "And please have Pippins ring Lady Davenport-Witt to invite her to join me."

"Yes, madam." Lizzie curtsied then left Ginger alone.

Boss sauntered over and poked Ginger's arm in search of a pat on the head and a scrub behind the ears.

"Oh, Bossy, you're a spoiled little brute, aren't you?

I'm afraid your life is about to change once again when this little one comes. Good thing you and Scout will have each other, as I may be a bit preoccupied for a while."

Ginger hadn't worn make-up for some time, but thought a trip down the corridor to the library, and with her out of her nightclothes, merited the effort. She winced as she plucked her eyebrows back into submission, creating the desired thin arches. Once her eyes stopped watering, she added blue eye shadow and brushed on mascara from a dark-brown pad. Two rosy spots added to her cheeks and tangerine lipstick to her lips, and she was finished. Her face was a bit rounder than she was used to, but it went with the roundness of everything else. As her father used to say, "This too shall pass."

Tempted to try a pair of shoes, Ginger shook her head. "Not worth the effort, nor the pain. Slippers will do just fine for Felicia." She slid her feet into her feather-topped slippers and shuffled away, with Boss on her heels.

The Hartigan House library was down the corridor from Ginger and Basil's bedroom, also facing the street side. A fire had been lit in the fireplace providing— along with shelves well stocked with a good selection of books—a cosy feel. The easel with the notes she and Felicia had made sat in the corner. Ginger lowered herself into one of the wingback chairs and stared at the notes and the list of suspects with the strongest motives written there. Archibald Foote, Virginia Foote, Patricia Foote, and now Murray Entwistle. And Humphrey.

Ginger mentally marked Archibald as the prime suspect, though finding her client's father guilty of murder would hardly be considered a win.

Felicia arrived in a fluster. "Charles wonders what I'm doing over here so often."

Ginger gave her a look. "You haven't told him you're working for me on this case?"

"Well, yes, but he thinks I'm just playing at it and wonders why I'm not taking matters at Witt House into my own hands." She flopped into a chair. "I'm the mistress now."

"Why are you not taking matters into your own hands?" Ginger asked. "This case isn't requiring all of your free time."

Felicia sighed. "I don't know. I'm just not motivated." She locked eyes with Ginger. "I need your help."

Felicia didn't have a mother or a mother-in-law who could step in and give guidance. Taking on the duties of such a grand residence as Witt House would indeed be very intimidating.

Ginger smiled sympathetically. "I'd be delighted to help. Witt House has waited this long for a mistress to put things in order," she said. "A few more weeks won't matter."

"Thank you, Ginger," Felicia said with a breath. "That's exactly what I think too."

Lizzie and Grace arrived with luncheon, and once the maids had gone, Ginger and Felicia dived in.

"I miss Mrs. Beasley's cooking," Felicia said after a bite. "Our cook is rather fussy, and the portions are piddling."

Ginger doubted there was a problem with the cook at Witt House. Felicia just seemed determined to find fault, however big or small.

Felicia's gaze landed on the easel. "Have we made any progress at all?"

Ginger sipped her tea. "At the moment, I think Archibald Foote is our most likely culprit."

"But?"

"It seems a little too tidy. All I really have on him is an overeagerness to be the man of the family. I've nothing to tie him to the actual crime."

"And Mr. Entwistle?"

"Same thing. I believe they'll be releasing him today, as they can't hold him without formalising the charge, and Basil doesn't think that will happen."

Felicia groaned. "We've hit a dead end."

"Did you happen to see Scout?" Ginger asked.

Felicia's head jerked at the change of subject. "Scout?"

"Yes. I know Mr. Fulton was taking him to a breeding stable this morning, but I half expected them to return. Scout uses the library for his lessons, and I don't want to infringe."

"I did see him, actually," Felicia said. "He was loitering about the front garden." Her lips pulled up slyly. "I think he was hoping for a sighting of Charlotte Foote."

Ginger smiled in return. "Quite likely."

Felicia got to her feet and stared outside.

"Is he there?" Ginger asked.

Felicia gasped. "No!" She turned to Ginger. "Charlotte just did the oddest thing. She threw her cat across the garden."

Ginger gaped. "Was the animal hurt?"

"It landed on all four feet then scurried into the hedge. I'm shocked at her cruel intentions."

Ginger frowned. "Perhaps we've been looking at this case all wrong."

Felicia returned to her seat and spoke with hushed seriousness. "You don't think a child did it, do you?"

A pit formed in Ginger's stomach. "Child murderers exist. Papers have been written on the phenomenon."

Felicia grimaced. "Oh mercy."

Ginger gave Felicia a pointed look. "I do believe that's my saying."

"And it was needed right at that moment." Crossing her legs, Felicia asked, "What do we do now?"

Ginger's mind went into high speed. All the pieces to this puzzle were there, but how did they fit together?

"Dr. Longden has been making covert house calls to the Foote residence. I wonder who his patient is."

Felicia raised a brow. "Charlotte?"

Ginger didn't answer. "How would you feel about calling on Dr. Longden to ask a few questions?"

"What, now? Won't he be at his surgery?"

"Go under the guise of making an appointment. Better yet, make an appointment."

"And what should I say is ailing me?"

"Make something up. Tell him you suspect you're with child."

Felicia blushed, then feigned a sniffle. "I do believe the common cold will do."

22

Though Felicia wouldn't admit to it, her stomach fluttered as she stepped into Dr. Longden's surgery, knowing she was entering into a bit of subterfuge. She chided herself at her silliness—it was perfectly natural for a lady to walk into a surgery and enquire of the resident physician, and this certainly wasn't her first time. Three patients sitting in padded chairs against one wall of the waiting room glanced up as she stepped inside, nodded politely, then returned their attention to the magazine or book with which they were engaged. One lady, wearing a brown cloche and a fur-trimmed wool coat, dropped her magazine and stared, mouth gaping as if she recognised Felicia. A subscriber to the social pages, Felicia mused. The Gold–Davenport-Witt wedding had made it into all the papers.

Felicia approached the receptionist, a middle-aged spinster named Miss Bird, whose facial features did well to reflect her surname—dark, deep-set eyes and a narrow, pointy nose.

On seeing Felicia, Miss Bird immediately put aside the paperwork she'd been attending to and stood. "Good day, Lady Davenport-Witt. So nice to see you again. I saw your wedding photograph in the newspaper. Such a happy time."

"Indeed, it was," Felicia said. "Thank you."

"Would you like to see Dr. Longden?" Miss Bird's eyes twinkled in conspiracy as if she, too, were guessing the reason for her visit, just as the lady in the brown cloche cleared her throat. How disappointed everyone would be in nine months when an announcement failed to appear!

"I don't want to disturb him if he's busy," Felicia said, aware that the people in the waiting room probably had an appointment. Knowing her title would gain her access anyway would've tickled her pink once upon a time, but at this moment, she didn't want to arouse extra attention. "In fact, I'm on my way to somewhere else, and when I saw I was near the surgery, I had my driver stop." Felicia had driven herself, having borrowed Ginger's Crossley at Ginger's insistence, but if she was playing a part, Felicia thought she'd better play it fully.

"I'd be happy to pencil you in for an appointment," Miss Bird said. Felicia chose a date and time that she had every intention of cancelling later on, then, keeping her voice low, brought up the Foote family. "They live on the same street as my dear friend Mrs. Reed. She's my former sister-in-law, but we're so much more than that. Yes, they're very excited about the new baby soon to arrive. Their son, Scout, has become friends with the youngest Foote daughter, Charlotte."

It was a bit of a stretch to claim a friendship between Scout and the girl he was soft on, but it gave her a way to bring the child's name into the conversation.

Just then, the door to Dr. Longden's office opened, and a woman holding the hand of a child walked out with Dr. Longden on her heels. Seeing Felicia seemed to startle him.

"Charlotte?" Miss Bird said. "Such a lovely name. Dr. Longden has a niece by that name. She often wrote him letters from Canada."

Canada? The mention of the country seemed to be coming up in conversation rather regularly of late.

"Though—" Miss Bird put a finger to her chin. "The letters have stopped recently. They came regularly once a month or so for the last four years."

Doctor Longden lived in a flat above the surgery, so it wasn't surprising that his personal post would come to Miss Bird. Before Felicia could ask more questions, Dr. Longden's voice reached her from behind.

"Lady Davenport-Witt? What a surprise."

Miss Bird cut in with Felicia's story of dropping in as she drove by to make an appointment for another time, but Dr. Longden insisted that he see to her now. He gave the three patients in the waiting room a look that begged for understanding. One must attend to the gentry first. It was expected.

Felicia claimed an empty chair as the doctor closed the door behind them. His consulting room was sparse, with a large desk sitting in front of a window and a bookshelf lined with medical textbooks and manuals. Nothing personal was apparent anywhere, not on the shelves, the desk, nor the walls. This was clearly a work-only space. Felicia glanced about, taking in all the details, wishing she knew what on earth it was she was hoping to see.

Dr. Longden sat on a stool in front of his desk, straightened his suit jacket and pushed up on his round spectacles. "Are you feeling under the weather, my lady?"

"A little. I think I have a cold. I've developed a nasty nasal headache." Felicia pinched the bridge of her nose for effect.

"I see," Dr. Longden said, looking unimpressed. Feeling she needed to modify the urgency of her ailments, she added, "And I've pulled a muscle in my arm. I'm redecorating Witt House, you see."

"Let's have a look at your throat, shall we?" the doctor said. "Say 'ah'."

Felicia complied with a feeble "Ah".

"Please hold out your arm."

Felicia did as instructed, feeling less enthused by her choice of subterfuge. The doctor rubbed and pinched her arm, the latter resulting in a heartfelt yelp.

The doctor scribbled something down on his pad of paper, then gave her a gentle look. "Are you having any feminine issues? Don't be shy, Lady Davenport-Witt. I've been a doctor for a long time and have seen and heard it all. I'm here to help you."

Lord have mercy! Felicia's cheeks flushed. She was so out of her realm here. Ginger would know what to do and execute it perfectly. Why had she agreed to come?

"Thank you, Dr. Longden," she managed to say. "I don't believe I'm in the family way at this time, but I'll come and see you the moment I suspect it. I'm afraid it's just a headache and a sore arm today."

"Very well. I'd suggest using aspirin to relieve your discomfort. It's available at any chemist."

Felicia must've looked as disheartened as she felt —she was failing in her mission! Then the doctor said, "I do have aspirin in the backroom to get you started.

If you don't mind waiting a moment, I'll fetch a bottle."

"That would be fabulous, Doctor," Felicia said.

The second the doctor left the room, Felicia jumped to her feet. She placed her handbag by the door, an early warning system of sorts, and hurried to the desk. The top was meticulous, with hardly an item out of place. Two trays, one labelled IN and one labelled OUT, were stacked and pushed to the far left side. A lone fountain pen occupied a pen holder.

Felicia's hands quivered as she opened the drawers, finding nothing of consequence, her heart beating as her eyes darted to the door. She had no idea what she hoped to find.

Until she found it.

In the bottom drawer was a stack of letters. The return address was from Canada, but the name attached wasn't from a person named Charlotte. Felicia gaped. These letters were from a Virginia Foote.

What were the doctor and Mrs. Foote corresponding about? Dare Felicia look at the contents? The most recent letter was on top. Felicia removed the single sheet of folded paper inside. Damning words jumped out at her as she scanned the page. *My beloved Warren. My heart aches to see you again. Your daughter . . . With lasting love, Virginia.*

Felicia jumped as her handbag shifted at the door. How she got the letter back into its envelope and in the drawer as fast as she did, she had no clue. She sprung to the window and gazed out, her hand on her hips.

Turning to the doctor, who stared perplexed at her handbag on the floor, Felicia said glibly. "I'm terribly sorry. My handbag's in your way. I didn't pay attention to where I dropped it. I just needed a breath of air. My sinuses, you see."

Dr. Longden blinked, then sighed. Felicia imagined the entitlement of the elite often tried the man's patience.

"It's quite all right, Lady Davenport-Witt," he said. He picked up her handbag and placed it on her vacated chair. "Forgive my tardiness. I had to take a telephone call." He held up a brown vial. "Here are your aspirin. Take two a day, and if your discomfort persists, please come and see me again."

Felicia accepted the small bottle of pills, dropped them into her handbag, then threw the straps over her shoulder.

"Thank you for seeing me at short notice, Dr. Longden," she said. Walking tall, she passed the aggravated patients still waiting, with the confidence and pride of a lady of her status. But when she finally got to the pearly-white Crossley, she remained in the red-leather driver's seat for several minutes before her nerves were calmed enough to drive.

Felicia's mind went to the letters Dr. Longden had received from Virginia Foote. She shook her head. What would Ginger think of this news? She started up the Crossley, grabbed the large steering wheel with two gloved hands, and roared back to Hartigan House.

23

*B*asil returned to Hartigan House in time to share dinner with Ginger, who had convinced him she was quite able to go down the stairs to the dining room, so long as she didn't go back up the stairs again before bedtime.

A long dark-wood table with matching chairs took up the length of the room. Above it hung an electric Tiffany lamp. Basil sat at one end, with Scout at his left elbow and Boss hiding under the lad's chair. Basil rose to pull out the chair to his right, helping Ginger get settled into it.

"I heard the police let Mr. Entwistle go," Scout said.

Ginger cast a startled look Basil's way, then at her son, and said, "Are you following the case?"

Scout lifted a shoulder. "It's hard not to when the

crime has happened across the street."

Ginger was quite certain his interest had something to do with young Charlotte. Normally, Scout was too focused on playing with Boss or riding the horses to concern himself with Ginger and Basil's work.

"Morris had to give him up," Basil said. "Not enough evidence. In fact, Entwistle's shoe print wasn't the only one found in the back garden that didn't belong to Mr. Foote, Humphrey, or the gardener, the only males beside Mr. Rothwell who'd have the right or reason to be back there. And Mr. Rothwell spent his time outside sitting in a chair."

"My guess is that the mystery footprint belongs to Dr. Longden," Ginger said.

Basil's fork paused mid-air. "Why do you say that?"

"I've seen him from our bedroom window," she answered. "I thought it odd that he'd use the back door instead of the front entrance. However, he is the Foote family doctor, so I suppose it's not so strange."

Scout's chin disappeared into his chest.

Ginger considered her son, then asked casually, "Have you seen Miss Charlotte lately?"

"No." He frowned. "She doesn't like dogs."

"Oh, poor Bossy," Ginger said.

Boss looked up hopefully at the sound of his name, and Ginger slipped him a piece of chicken.

"Boss and I are a team," Scout said with a note of

defiance.

"Good going, son," Basil said. "I respect a man of principle."

Scout beamed at the validation, and Ginger wanted to hug Basil for making Scout feel proud.

Basil cut into his chicken thigh. "Mr. Foote and his man Humphrey came to the Yard today."

Ginger lowered her fork. "Is that so? Whatever for?"

"Each to provide the other with an alibi."

"How convenient."

"I thought so too. Mr. Foote claims he had an urgent meeting with his tailor and, at short notice, engaged Humphrey to drive him. The outing happened while Rothwell was still alive. There weren't at the house when Charlotte had her turn with her grandfather."

"And the tailor confirms this?"

Basil nodded. "He does and has a receipt to prove that the hemming was done in a timely manner."

"So, he and Humphrey didn't drive to another street, park, slip back in the lane behind the Foote residence, climb into the window to remain unseen, and kill Mr. Rothwell?"

"No, they did not."

Voices from the entry hall reached them, and soon, Felicia breezed into the dining room. "Pippins told me

I could find you in here." She grinned at Basil. "You let her come down the stairs, did you?"

"As you know, Ginger can present a very convincing case when she wants to," he said.

Felicia laughed. "That I do."

"That's enough banter on my account," Ginger said lightly. "Felicia, you'll join us for dinner?"

"If you don't mind. Charles is working late tonight, and I am rather famished."

Felicia gave Scout a quick shoulder hug before taking the empty seat beside him.

Lizzie and Grace arrived with more roast chicken, potatoes, and green beans, and once Felicia had taken enough bites to stave off her hunger, she caught Ginger's eye.

"Can I presume your visit to the surgery was eventful?" Ginger said.

"Quite." Felicia glanced at Scout, shot Ginger and Basil a questioning look, which led to Ginger and Basil eyeing each other. Should they talk about the case in front of Scout?

Scout, proving to be quite intuitive for his age, shifted in his seat. "Shall I ask to be excused?"

"Have you had enough to eat?" Ginger asked.

"Mrs. Beasley has biscuits in the kitchen," Scout returned. "And perhaps a bone for Boss."

"Very well," Basil started, "you may be excused."

Ginger watched as Scout and Boss disappeared behind the dining room door, then turned to Felicia. "Please, do tell."

"Dr. Longden and Mrs. Foote are lovers, and Charlotte is their love child!"

Ginger gaped as Felicia stared across the table with a definite look of triumph on her face.

"You didn't see that one coming," she added with a note of glee, "did you?"

"I did not," Ginger said. She turned to Basil. "Did you know about this?"

Basil shook his head. "No. I'm stunned. Felicia, how did you come across this information?"

"I had a little peek in Dr. Longden's desk when he left to get me a bottle of aspirin. There was a pile of letters from Virginia Foote with a Canadian return address. I had a quick look at the last letter. I didn't have time to read it thoroughly, but something was mentioned about a daughter and Charlotte's name as well."

Even her babe seemed impressed by bold move and Ginger held her belly where the child kicked.

"Did it specifically say that Charlotte was their child?" Basil asked.

Felicia's shoulders slumped. "I didn't see that, exactly. I only had a brief moment to peruse the letter, and actually, the receptionist believes Dr. Longden has a niece by that name. But—" She sat up straight once again. "—the tone was definitely amorous."

Ginger pursed her lips. "This sheds new light on things. It explains why Dr. Longden has been sneaking about the Foote residence."

"He's trying to see his daughter without Mr. Foote knowing," Felicia said.

"And possibly trying to protect her," Ginger added, "perhaps by interfering with evidence."

Basil stiffened. "Protect her? Do you suspect a thirteen-year-old girl of murder?"

"I'm saying we can't rule her out because of her age," Ginger said. "Felicia witnessed heartless behaviour from Miss Charlotte towards her cat."

"That hardly makes her a murderer," Basil said, though his voice lacked its former confidence.

"Clearly," Ginger agreed, "but it shows the capacity to harm others. I just don't think it would be wise to ignore her as a suspect because of her age."

"I concur." Basil pushed away from the table. "I think it's time I chatted with Miss Charlotte Foote."

Ginger so desperately wanted to go with him, but, accepting her fate, did the next best thing. "Take Felicia with you," she said. "She'll help put the child at ease."

Basil flashed a knowing grin. "Anything for you, my love."

elicia was fully aware that she'd been sent with Basil to be Ginger's eyes and ears and that Basil was putting up with her when it was in his right to tell her to keep her nose out of things.

"I'm only going to make subtle enquiries," Basil explained as they drew closer to the front door of the Foote residence. He held a black umbrella, large enough to protect the two of them from the constant rain.

"I'll keep my thoughts to myself," Felicia said. "You're the lead."

Basil seemed to relax at her deference. They stood on the doorstep as Basil rang the bell.

Soon afterwards, Humphrey answered. With barely concealed contempt, he said, "Good evening, sir, my lady."

"We're sorry to intrude, but it is rather important that I speak to Mrs. Foote. Is she at home?"

"I'll see if she's available," Humphrey said, and since he could hardly expect Felicia to wait outside in the rain, he motioned for them to step into the entrance hall, the gas lamps burning dimly. Felicia thought if she were the lady of the house, the first thing she'd do would be to have electricity brought to the residence. In these modern times, there really wasn't any excuse.

Humphrey returned. "Mrs. Foote will see you in the sitting room. Please follow me."

Poor Mrs. Foote wore her distress like a cloak. Dark circles under her eyes were proof she hadn't slept well since her father had died.

"Tea is on its way," she said cheerlessly. "With this dreary weather, I know I could use a cup."

Felicia and Basil settled into the matching armchairs, while Mrs. Foote sat on one end of the settee.

"I suppose you're here because of Mr. Entwistle's release," Mrs. Foote said stiffly. "Just because the man has been set free, doesn't mean he's not guilty."

"Do you believe him to be guilty, Mrs. Foote?" Basil asked.

Surprisingly, Mrs. Foote hesitated. "I admit, the whole thing has been exasperating and exhausting.

Father never could do anything without creating drama, not even in his death." She sighed. "For Patricia's sake, I hope Mr. Entwistle is innocent. Either way, the scandal must put an end to the engagement."

"Does Miss Foote feel that way?" Felicia asked.

"She hardly has a choice now," Mrs. Foote said. "We're certainly not paying for a wedding."

It was the maid Abby who brought the tea. She set the tray on the tea table, curtsied, and asked, "Is there anything else, madam?"

"Please keep an eye on Miss Charlotte for me, will you?"

Another curtsey. "Yes, madam."

Basil lifted a finger. "Actually, I wouldn't mind if Miss Charlotte joined us."

Mrs. Foote stared back at him, aghast. "Whatever for?"

"She was present on the day Mr. Rothwell died, was she not?" Basil said gently. "I'd be remiss not to ask her what she saw. Children can be very perceptive."

It was clear to Felicia that Mrs. Foote's feathers were ruffled, but she could hardly decline the request of a chief inspector at Scotland Yard.

"Abby," she started, "find Miss Charlotte and bring her to me."

There was an awkward period of tea sipping

between the three, and then Miss Charlotte finally arrived, accompanied by Miss Patricia Foote.

"Oh good," Basil said lightly. "Miss Foote, do join us."

"I believe I will," Miss Foote said. She took the end of the settee opposite her mother while Charlotte was left with the middle. The youngest Foote family member sat stiffly, her hands in her lap, fussing with the pleats of her skirt. Her hair was brushed smooth and pinned off her face, but her eyes, Felicia hadn't noticed the colour before, were dark blue, and stared blankly ahead.

"You must be relieved at Mr. Entwistle's release, Miss Foote," Basil said.

"Of course," Miss Foote returned stiffly.

"And you, Mrs. Foote, now that Mr. Foote has produced a solid alibi, along with Humphrey."

Mrs. Foote scowled. "What exactly are you getting at, Chief Inspector?"

"Only that all the male suspects have been exonerated." Basil placed an elbow on his knee and leaned in. "That leaves the three of you."

Mrs. Foote jumped to her feet. "That's outrageous!"

Basil stood, placing a palm up. "Please, Mrs. Foote. Do sit down. We'll get to the bottom of this, eventually."

Mrs. Foote smoothed out her skirt and patted at the base of her mousy-brown bob before retaking her seat. She helped herself to a sip of tea, and Felicia noticed the lady's hand quivering slightly.

"Miss Charlotte," Basil began. "You were the last to see your grandfather alive, were you not?"

Charlotte cast a nervous glance at her mother, who came to her defence once again. "You're frightening her."

Felicia wouldn't peg the emotion she saw behind Charlotte's eyes, enlarged by the thick spectacles she wore, as fear but rage.

Basil directed his response to Miss Charlotte. "It's not my intention to frighten you, Miss Charlotte, simply to better understand the situation. What was your relationship with your grandfather like?"

Miss Charlotte, so steely eyed for one so young, said, "I hated him."

Mrs. Foote gasped, and Felicia admitted to joining in. The child's vitriol was so unexpected.

Basil's gaze landed on Mrs. Foote. Her daughter had just professed motive. And being the last to see Mr. Rothwell alive, she had means and opportunity.

Miss Foote inhaled deeply, stuck out her chin as she stared at Basil, then took Miss Charlotte's hand. "Chief Inspector Reed, if you've come for a confession, you'll have it. I killed my grandfather."

Miss Charlotte squealed, "No, it was me!"

Miss Foote tugged on Charlotte's arm. "Stop it, Char." Then to Basil, she said, "Arrest me. I did it."

Mrs. Foote, red in the face with eyes of fury, was back on her feet. "This is nonsense! Chief Inspector, I killed my father. My daughters are only trying to protect me."

Felicia's neck ached from whipping it between all the suspects and their confessions. Ginger was going to be so cross at missing this display!

Basil remained seated, waved for Mrs. Foote to sit, then casually crossed his legs. "It appears we are at an impasse. Either one of you killed Mr. Rothwell, or you all worked together."

A chorus of dissent followed. "No!"

Patricia Foote remained insistent. "I tell you, I worked alone. It was me."

With a glint in her eye, Charlotte echoed, "I worked alone. It was me."

Basil once again raised a palm in Virginia Foote's direction. "Please, it's unnecessary for you to express your confession again as well."

Felicia was flabbergasted. They went from no known killers to three persons taking credit, each undermining the effectiveness of the others. Perhaps that was their intention.

"Obviously, one of you is the guilty party," Basil

said, "and the other two believe they are protecting the guilty by claiming the guilt for themselves. I commend your joining ranks, but what I don't understand is why there was need to kill an old man who hadn't long left on this earth. Was he about to change the will?"

Virginia Foote laughed mirthlessly. "I couldn't care less about that blasted will. In the end, Father had made it clear he was never going to give a penny to my daughters or me, so whatever changes he made to it wouldn't affect us."

Basil persisted. "Why then?" When none of the Foote ladies answered, he turned to Miss Charlotte. "Why did you hate your grandfather?"

Miss Charlotte spat, "He was a bossy, despicable old man!"

Miss Foote chortled, "He was boorish to us all. Until he had his first stroke, which put him in his chair, he overpowered us all." Miss Foote's hand flung wide, indicating Mr. Rothwell's abrasive behaviour went to Mrs. Foote as well. "Emotionally and financially. We were at his mercy."

She smiled smugly. "When it appeared that he was having another stroke—I know it was heart failure now —I simply helped him along."

Charlotte shook her head. "Patricia, please. Don't lie for me. It was I who helped him along."

Mrs. Foote blurted out, "No! I'm the killer. I

should've shielded my daughters from his malevolent, spiteful ways. I hated my father and couldn't wait to send him off to Hades." She stared at Felicia and Basil defiantly, holding out her wrists dramatically. "You can take me now."

25

Ginger, Basil, and Felicia gathered in the sitting room. Ginger could hardly believe her ears when Basil and Felicia told their tale.

"They *all* confessed?"

"Mrs. Foote, if she's not the murderer, is attempting to protect one of her daughters," Basil said.

"Patricia had the strongest motive," Felicia suggested. "True love can drive one to madness. I don't know what I'd do if someone tried to keep me from Charles."

"And I hate to be uncharitable," Ginger started, "but Charlotte Foote seems to lack a soul."

"There have been cases involving violent children that have baffled doctors," Basil said.

Felicia turned to him. "Could a young girl like that

have the strength to suffocate a man? He was infirm but not crippled."

"In the grip of strong excitement," Basil said, "yes, I believe she could. But we could hypothesise all day. The problem is, we don't have any evidence."

Ginger closed her eyes, musing like her new fictional friend, Poirot. This was a problem. She must engage her grey cells.

"Ginger?" Felicia prompted. "Do you have an idea?"

"I do," she said, but before she could present it, she let out an involuntary yelp.

"Are you all right, love?" Basil asked, concern written on his face.

Ginger held her belly, which was tightening again. "Just another Braxton Hicks. No need to be alarmed." The tension passed, and Ginger let out a long breath.

"Your idea?" Felicia asked again.

"We need to set a trap of some kind," Ginger offered.

Basil leaned in with interest. "And what do you propose?"

"What if we put word out that a witness to the crime has come forward," Ginger started. "Or better yet, if the 'witness' asked for blackmail money. That could sift them out."

"Even if it's Charlotte?" Felicia asked. "I expect

she'd go to Patricia for help, and that would muddy the waters again."

Ginger rubbed the bridge of her nose, thinking. "We need bait. A real witness."

"Abby?" Basil said. "She'd lose her position."

"Then we'll take her on here," Ginger said. "We could use more staff."

"Do you think she'd agree to it?" Felicia asked.

"She doesn't seem to be the kind of woman who'd want to aid a murderer, much less work for one," Ginger said. "I suppose we won't know unless we ask." Keeping her gaze on Felicia, she continued, "Would you mind summoning her? Use Lizzie if need be."

Felicia nodded as she got to her feet and left the sitting room.

Ginger smiled at Basil. "Perhaps I'll type up the letters. Shall we ask the murderer to meet us in Kensington Gardens? It's walking distance, and if Miss Charlotte is our killer, she will be able to get there on foot."

Basil chuckled. "Not *us*, my love. My men and I will be stationed there."

"Of course," Ginger said. "Slip of the tongue. I'll draft the letters so only the real killer will respond to the threat. Miss Charlotte won't have access to cash, but perhaps Abby can recommend a family heirloom she could get her hands on."

Basil helped Ginger to her feet and walked with her to the study at the back of the house. "Have the killer drop a handbag under the bench near the Albert Memorial tomorrow afternoon at one. I'll arrange for my constables to be ready."

Ginger settled into her office chair and rolled a plain sheet of paper into the black high-back typewriter. "I'll let you know when the letters have been delivered."

Basil kissed her on the head. "And when you've done this, please, I beg of you, put your feet up and rest. Or better yet, go to bed."

"I will, love," Ginger said, her eyes on the typewriter. "I promise."

Once Basil had left, Ginger worked on the first letter, starting with Mrs. Foote.

I know what you did.

I have proof.

I'll do you a favour, if you do one for me. A hundred pounds to keep me quiet. It's a small price to pay to avoid the noose, wouldn't you say?

Drop a handbag with the money under the bench by the Albert Memorial in Kensington Gardens at one p.m. today.

Come alone.

I'll be watching.

Do it, or I go to the police.

Would that do it? Anyone but the killer would think the letter a hoax. What kind of proof could someone have? But the killer would want to be sure.

Satisfied with her prose, Ginger removed the sheet, folded it into thirds, and placed the letter inside after typing VF on the envelope. She then sealed the glue with a damp sponge.

Felicia entered Ginger's study the next morning with Abby in tow. Ginger welcomed them both, then motioned to the empty chairs in front of her desk. "Abby, please have a seat."

Abby curtsied. "Yes, madam," she said, then did as instructed. Felicia took the remaining chair, sitting upright with gloved hands folded on her lap.

"Did Lady Davenport-Witt have a chance to explain why we've asked you to come?"

Felicia answered for her. "I thought it best if it came from you."

"Of course." To Abby, she began, "I have an enormous request to make of you, and I hope you'll consider it seriously before replying."

"Yes, madam, I always consider everything seriously."

"Very good. Lady Davenport-Witt and I are cooperating with the police to find Mr. Rothwell's killer. Unfortunately, it appears that his death may have been at the hands of a member of the Foote family. To smoke the guilty person out, we're setting a little trap, you could say."

"I see, madam."

"What I'm asking is for you to deliver an envelope to each of the Foote ladies, clandestinely, so that they don't see you or each other when they find the letter."

"I see, madam," Abby said again. Her lips pursed.

Ginger respected her for not shrinking in her seat. "Will you do it?" Ginger asked.

"I believe in justice, madam, though it grieves me to think one of my ladies could be responsible for this grievous deed."

"It includes a letter to Miss Charlotte."

Abby's hand went to her heart, but she didn't, as Ginger had hoped, protest at the possibility that a child who'd been in her care could be responsible for such a terrible deed. She cast a glance at Felicia as they waited.

Abby finally gave words to her thoughts. "I understand, madam."

"We realise that this is a lot to ask and that you are endangering your livelihood, and if things are as dangerous as we fear, even your life. To that end, I would like to offer you a position at Hartigan House, should you desire to work here."

Abby brightened. "I've only heard good things

from the staff here, madam, and it would be a pleasure to work for you."

"Very good," Ginger said. "Now, I need a little information from you. Is there an heirloom or item of value that Miss Charlotte could obtain as a request from a would-be blackmailer?"

"There's a small clock on the mantel in the drawing room, madam. It dates back to the seventeenth century." Abby glanced at her lap. "I do hope it's not the child, madam."

Ginger stared at the maid with compassion. "I hope not too, Abby."

Checking her watch, Ginger said, "Oh, look at the time." She put a third sheet of paper into her typewriter and quickly typed out a letter for Charlotte, substituting the priceless clock for the money. When she'd completed stuffing the remaining two envelopes, she gave them to Abby. "Do be careful. Stealth and discretion are much needed."

Abby accepted the envelopes, then curtsied. "I will, madam. I hope you find your killer."

"I'll be heading to Kensington Gardens, as well," Felicia said.

Ginger pursed her lips. "It could be dangerous."

Felicia scoffed. "I'm your eyes and ears, remember? You can't seriously tell me you're willing to wait until

Basil has a chance to report back to find out who turns up at the park?"

Ginger relented. "Yes, go, but stay out of sight. Better yet, wear a disguise!"

Felicia laughed. "I'll don a red wig and pretend to be you."

When Felicia had gone, Ginger returned to her typewriter, typed up another brief letter, folded it, and placed it in an envelope. She then rang the bell for Pippins.

Her faithful butler soon arrived, his blue eyes wide with expectation, one arm behind his long, slightly stooped back. "You rang, madam?"

Ginger held out the envelope. "I'm hoping you'll do me a favour." Ginger relayed the address. "I'd appreciate your discretion."

"Of course, madam," Pippins said with a slight bow. "Always."

26

To think that she'd only moved to London three years previously, during a restless and rowdy time in her life. At that time, Felicia thought she'd be stuck in the small village of Chesterton forever. The Gold family home of Bray Manor had suffered a fire, and if it hadn't been for Ginger and her hospitality, she and Grandmama would still be living in the remaining smoke-damaged wing. Felicia wouldn't have met Charles, and she wouldn't have moved from her childish way into a lady of repute—at least not as seamlessly as she had. Felicia had much to thank Ginger for.

This was why Felicia desperately wanted to succeed in all the important investigative tasks Ginger had given her, tasks that Ginger would've done herself under other circumstances. Felicia tucked her chin into the fur collar of her wool coat and continued along the path.

On a warm and sunny day, Kensington Gardens was filled with strollers and picnickers, crowds with which one could easily mix. At least the drizzling rain allowed for an umbrella, a barrier to conceal one's identity. Felicia was now well known in London society, and had she walked about in her typical fashion, she was sure to have been stopped and chatted to.

Today, however, pedestrians didn't meander but rather walked briskly, heads tucked under umbrellas, their purpose merely to cross through the park and reach their ultimate destination and not mosey about to enjoy the roses.

It made surveillance difficult. The last thing Felicia wanted was to distract the killer when she arrived. She'd simply have to walk slower to the park's south edge where the Albert Memorial was situated.

She wasn't the only one. Felicia made note of plain-clothed constables, recognising the handsome face of Brian Braxton. She felt a pang of remorse regarding the way she'd trifled with his feelings. It amazed her how marriage to Charles had catapulted her into maturity, and when she looked back at her behaviour, it made her blush with embarrassment.

The past was the past. She was a new lady now, an

actual Lady, and she would rise to the respect her station asked of her.

Having spotted the constables, Felicia looked for Basil. Surely, he wouldn't have set his men up and stayed behind.

The whinny of a horse caught her attention, and she smiled as she recognised the Arabian—Sir Blackwell—and his owner mounted on his back. She gave a subtle nod to Basil but kept strolling.

The bench was in sight. Felicia checked her wristwatch, and her heart leapt as she noted the time. Only one minute left, and the killer would hopefully be revealed. Felicia turned on her heel and headed in the other direction.

One other lone stroller, a stranger, approached the bench, and Felicia worried the man would sit down. Would his presence derail their plans and frighten off their target? What rotten timing!

Thankfully, the damp surface deterred the man, and he continued without taking a seat. Felicia's heart raced as she continued to wait. Would anyone show up, and if so, who?

And then, out of the corner of her eye, she saw a member of the Foote family walk along the park's path, a dark handbag strapped over one shoulder.

Felicia pinched her eyes shut, suppressing her distress.

It was Miss Charlotte.

Felicia had honestly believed it would be Miss Foote who appeared or Mrs. Foote, but here the child, with an oversized umbrella, pale face, and defiant eyes, delivered her parcel.

It had been agreed upon, should Charlotte be the one who responded to the letter, that the police would not make a public arrest. Felicia, along with Basil and the constables, stayed in their positions. Basil's gaze held a deep sadness.

Charlotte disappeared, but before her handbag could be retrieved, another person approached the bench, head ducked, with a bulky bag tucked under one arm.

There was no missing those thick round spectacles.

Dr. Longden had fallen into the trap.

*G*inger considered her small audience, who surrounded her as she once again lay on her bed. Basil and Felicia stared down at her in wonder, and Matilda, seated by the window, watched with a glint of concern in her eyes.

"How did you know?" Felicia asked.

Ginger reached for Basil's hand. "Did Dr. Longden confess?"

"Indeed. Poor chap, having vowed to only do good and not harm, and keeping that vow for his whole life until now, buckled under the strain of it."

"But why?" This came from Matilda, who placed a hand over her lips. "I'm sorry. I spoke out of turn."

"It's quite all right," Ginger said. "I'm sure this has come as a shock to you."

"It has," Matilda admitted. "I've helped the doctor

deliver many babies. He's never been anything but respectful of everyone he's ever encountered." Matilda rubbed at the lines that had formed on her forehead. "I just don't understand."

"Although Dr. Longden never married," Basil began, "he had fallen in love. However, the object of his affection was already married."

"Mrs. Foote," Matilda supplied.

"Yes," Basil said. "And a daughter was produced from that love affair. Charlotte."

"And no one ever knew?" Felicia asked. "No one suspected?"

Basil pulled up the second chair and offered it to Felicia. She accepted.

"Dr. Longden and Mrs. Foote were determined to protect the child's reputation, no matter what," Basil continued. "Though they remained in love, he claims that no intimacy has occurred between them since Charlotte's birth."

"Only love letters," Felicia said.

"He insists the letters were to keep him informed of Charlotte's life and development. He despaired at the separation and rejoiced when Mr. Foote's job in Canada ended, and they returned. Charlotte's poor eyesight gave them a medical reason to meet, more than necessary perhaps, but Dr. Longden thought that he and Mrs. Foote could successfully continue the ruse."

"Until?" Ginger prompted.

"Until the day of Mr. Rothwell's demise," Basil said. "Crispin Rothwell, though physically frail, was mentally sharp. He took note of the extra doctor's visits and quite likely the affection between the doctor and Mrs. Foote—well exceeding a normal doctor-patient relationship. And when Charlotte got her spectacles, he saw the similarity.

"He confronted Virginia, and Charlotte overheard." Basil exhaled as if bracing himself to reveal something distasteful. "It was Charlotte who held the cushion over Mr. Rothwell's face."

Felicia gasped. "No."

Basil nodded grimly. "She believed Rothwell had passed away, but the effort had only caused him to pass out. Charlotte ran out of the room, leaving the cushion behind."

Ginger squirmed in her bed. "And Virginia Foote also believed her father had died?"

"Yes, seeing Charlotte flee the room, she went inside, then, on noting her father's stillness, immediately summoned Warren Longden. She hadn't noticed the blood on the cushion that came from her father's nosebleed."

"So, Mr. Rothwell was still alive when the doctor arrived?" Matilda asked.

"According to the doctor's confession, he was

alive," Basil said, "and barely conscious. With his natural tenacity, he told Longden that Charlotte had tried to kill him and that he was going to let everyone know that he and Virginia had birthed a devil child."

"Then Dr. Longden finished the job his daughter had started," Ginger said, seeing the picture form. "He's the person who attempted to burn the cushion."

"That is his confession," Basil said, "though I'd think he'd have means to a more sophisticated way to extinguish his patient. Perhaps a dose of morphine."

"He mightn't have carried enough morphine in his bag to kill Mr. Rothwell," Ginger said. "And an injection and overdose could be discovered by a savvy pathologist. We have to remember that he acted under duress, panicked enough to break his vow to do no harm."

"I suppose so," Basil conceded. "It'll be left to the courts to decide what happens to him."

Ginger let out a deep groan.

Basil jumped to his feet. "Ginger?"

Matilda joined them at the bed, and Ginger explained. "I had my suspicions about Dr. Longden, so had Pippins ring for Matilda." She squeezed Basil's hand. "I don't think these are Braxton Hicks, love. I believe I'm in labour."

*S*now fell in a soft, quiet blanket, frosting Mallowan Court in a pure crystal-white. Ginger, with baby Rosa at her breast, rocked in the chair by the bedroom window. It had been two weeks since Matilda had helped Ginger bring this miracle into the world, and Ginger couldn't stop staring at her little daughter in wonder. And gratitude. She had done what her own mother had not been able to do—survive the birth and delight in the prospect of a wonderful future raising her baby.

"There's nothing like an infant to revive one," Ambrosia said from her position in one of the gold-and-white-striped armchairs. Ginger had to agree with Ambrosia's statement, in fact, the dowager herself looked younger to Ginger, as if she had a renewed purpose to stick around this earth a mite longer.

Felicia sat opposite her grandmother and stared at Ginger wistfully. "You're a terrific mother, Ginger."

Ginger stroked the dark hair on her baby's head. "You will be, too, when the time comes."

Felicia laughed. "I'm in no hurry. I love sleeping too much."

As if triggered by the word "sleep", Ginger yawned. "It helps to have a capable nanny."

Ginger had been true to her word and had given Abby a job, but when she'd seen how natural she was with Rosa, competently changing her nappies and cooing her to sleep, she'd employed her as the nanny. Abby had even brought Rosa a gift, a new children's book called *Winnie-the-Pooh*.

Soon the baby would feed with bottles only, and Ginger would be free to return to her work at Feathers & Flair as much as she liked. Though, it wouldn't be as easy as she'd thought. This little baby held her heartstrings tightly in her little fist.

Felicia picked up the Agatha Christie book that Ginger had read while on bedrest. She laid it down again, then walked to the window and stared at the now-empty house across the street. She said, "I can't believe the doctor did it."

Ginger's lips twitched at the irony. If she ever had the privilege of meeting Mrs. Christie one day—

The last of the Foote belongings were currently

being removed by hired men. As it turned out, Mr. Rothwell had changed his will to favour his daughter, Virginia Foote, and Ginger assumed both granddaughters would continue to receive the allowances to which they'd become accustomed.

"I heard from Mrs. Schofield that Mrs. Foote plans to return to Canada with Miss Charlotte," Ambrosia said.

"Perhaps to protect her daughter from the ongoing public attention," Ginger remarked. "I hope she'll get the help she needs there."

"I wonder if Miss Foote, rather Mrs. Entwistle, has found happiness," Felicia added, "now that we have fulfilled our duties and cleared their names."

Ginger wondered that too. Patricia Foote had wasted no time in marrying Mr. Entwistle, eloping at Gretna Green in Scotland and settling there. Mr. Foote had moved into a London hotel, waiting for the divorce to finalize.

Felicia's gaze remained fixed out the window. "And what's going to happen to the house?"

Ginger threw a towel over her shoulder and rested tiny Rosa there. She patted the baby's back and said, "I don't know. Someone else will take it over."

Felicia spun around and stared at Ginger with wide eyes. "What if Charles and I moved into it?"

Ambrosia blinked in astonishment. "Are you serious? What about Witt House? You're the lady of the manor!"

"I know, Grandmama, but Witt House is too big. I feel lost in it. And with Charles working so often, I feel too far away from you and Ginger. And now, little Rosa."

Excitement stirred in Ginger's belly. "Do you think Charles will go for it?"

"I don't see why not. It's not like he has to sell Witt House. Before I came into his life, he rarely spent time there anyway." She turned to stare at the house on the other side of Mallowan Court and beamed. "We could decorate it together, Ginger. Bring it into the twentieth century." Spinning back to Ginger, she added, "We would be neighbours."

"I think it's a grand idea," Ginger said with sincerity. "And I, too, think I was already worried about how much I'd miss you."

Discuss the books, ask questions, share your opinions. Fun giveaways! Join the Lee Strauss Readers' Group on Facebook for more info.

Read on for what's next!

If you enjoyed reading *Murder on Mallowan Court* please help others enjoy it too.

Recommend it: Help others find the book by recommending it to friends, readers' groups, discussion boards and by **suggesting it to your local library.**

Review it: Please tell other readers why you liked this book by reviewing it on Amazon or Goodreads.

* No spoilers please *

Don't miss the next Ginger Gold mystery~
MURDER AT THE SAVOY

Murder's frightfully unlucky!

Mrs. Ginger Reed, known also as Lady Gold, settles into home life with her husband Chief Inspector Basil Reed, son Scout and newborn daughter Rosa, but when an opportunity to join a dinner party at the renown Savoy Hotel if offered, she's eager to engage in a carefree night with friends. Some of the guests are troubled when their party's number lands at unlucky thirteen, as death is sure to come to the first person who leaves the table.

Thankfully, the Savoy has an answer to this superstitious dilemma. A small statue of a black cat fondly known as Kaspar is given the empty seat, rounding the number to fourteen.

Unfortunately, in this instance Kaspar didn't fulfil his duties and a murder is committed. The case is tricky and complicated by a recent escape of a prisoner who has a bone to pick with Basil. Are the two seemingly unrelated incidents connected?

Ginger and Basil work together to solve one while avoiding the other, and what can they do about the black cat who crossed their path?

Buy on AMAZON or read Free with Kindle Unlimited!   .

1920S COLORING BOOK

Adult coloring book for lovers of 1920s fashion and lore. Original sketches by artist Joel Strauss. Commentary by Lee Strauss.

Have you discovered Rosa Reed?
Check out this new, fun 1950s cozy mystery series!

MURDER AT HIGH TIDE
a Rosa Reed Mystery #1

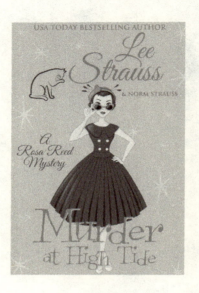

Murder's all wet!

It's 1956 and WPC (Woman Police Constable) Rosa Reed has left her groom at the altar in London. Time spent with her American cousins in Santa Bonita, California is exactly what she needs to get back on her feet, though the last thing she expected was to get entangled in another murder case!

If you love early rock & roll, poodle skirts, clever who-dun-its, a charming cat and an even more charming detective, you're going to love this new series!

Buy on AMAZON or read Free with Kindle Unlimited!
Available on Barnes & Noble and Book Depository

GINGER GOLD'S JOURNAL

Sign up for Lee's readers list and gain access to **Ginger Gold's private Journal.** Find out about Ginger's Life before the SS *Rosa* and how she became the woman she has. This is a fluid document that will cover her romance with her late husband Daniel, her time serving in the British secret service during World War One, and beyond. Includes a recipe for Dark Dutch Chocolate Cake!

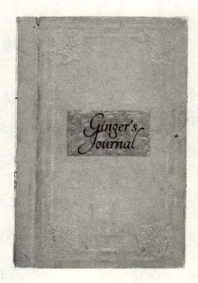

It begins: **July 31, 1912**

How fabulous that I found this Journal today, hidden in the bottom of my wardrobe. Good old Pippins, our English butler in London, gave it to me as a parting gift when Father whisked me away on our American adventure so he could marry Sally. Pips said it was for me to record my new adventures. I'm ashamed I never even penned one word before today. I think I was just too sad.

This old leather-bound journal takes me back to that emotional time. I had shed enough tears to fill the ocean and I remember telling Father dramatically that I was certain to cause flooding to match God's. At eight years old I was well-trained in my biblical studies, though, in retro-spect, I would say that I had probably bordered on heresy with my little tantrum.

The first week of my "adventure" was spent with a tummy ache and a number of embarrassing sessions that involved a bucket and Father holding back my long hair so I wouldn't soil it with vomit.

I certainly felt that I was being punished for some reason. Hartigan House—though large and sometimes lonely—was my home and Pips was my good friend. He often helped me to pass the time with games of I Spy and Xs and Os.

"Very good, Little Miss," he'd say with a twinkle in his blue eyes when I won, which I did often. I suspect now that our good butler wasn't beyond letting me win even when unmerited.

Father had got it into his silly head that I needed a mother, but I think the truth was he wanted a wife. Sally, a woman half my father's age, turned out to be a sufficient wife in the end, but I could never claim her as a mother.

Well, Pips, I'm sure you'd be happy to

know that things turned out all right here in America.

SUBSCRIBE to read more!
http://www.
leestraussbooks.com/gingergoldjournalsignup/

.

MORE FROM LEE STRAUSS

On AMAZON

GINGER GOLD MYSTERY SERIES (cozy 1920s historical)

Cozy. Charming. Filled with Bright Young Things. This Jazz Age murder mystery will entertain and delight you with its 1920s flair and pizzazz!

Murder on the SS Rosa

Murder at Hartigan House

Murder at Bray Manor

Murder at Feathers & Flair

Murder at the Mortuary

Murder at Kensington Gardens

Murder at St. George's Church

The Wedding of Ginger & Basil

Murder Aboard the Flying Scotsman

Murder at the Boat Club

Murder on Eaton Square

Murder by Plum Pudding

Murder on Fleet Street

Murder at Brighton Beach

Murder in Hyde Park

Murder at the Royal Albert Hall

Murder in Belgravia

Murder on Mallowan Court

Murder at the Savoy

LADY GOLD INVESTIGATES (Ginger Gold companion short stories)

Volume 1

Volume 2

Volume 3

Volume 4

HIGGINS & HAWKE MYSTERY SERIES (cozy 1930s historical)

The 1930s meets Rizzoli & Isles in this friendship depression era cozy mystery series.

Death at the Tavern

Death on the Tower

Death on Hanover

Death by Dancing

THE ROSA REED MYSTERIES

(1950s cozy historical)

Murder at High Tide

Murder on the Boardwalk

Murder at the Bomb Shelter

Murder on Location

Murder and Rock 'n Roll

Murder at the Races

Murder at the Dude Ranch

Murder in London

Murder at the Fiesta

A NURSERY RHYME MYSTERY SERIES (mystery/sci fi)

Marlow finds himself teamed up with intelligent and savvy Sage Farrell, a girl so far out of his league he feels blinded in her presence - literally - damned glasses! Together they work to find the identity of @gingerbreadman. Can they stop the killer before he strikes again?

Gingerbread Man

Life Is but a Dream

Hickory Dickory Dock

Twinkle Little Star

THE PERCEPTION TRILOGY (YA dystopian mystery)

Zoe Vanderveen is a GAP—a genetically altered person. She lives in the security of a walled city on prime water-front property along side other equally beautiful people with extended life spans. Her brother Liam is missing. Noah Brody, a boy on the outside, is the only one who can help ~ but can she trust him?

Perception

Volition

Contrition

LIGHT & LOVE (sweet romance)

Set in the dazzling charm of Europe, follow Katja, Gabriella, Eva, Anna and Belle as they find strength, hope and love.

Sing me a Love Song

Your Love is Sweet

In Light of Us

Lying in Starlight

PLAYING WITH MATCHES (WW2 history/romance)

A sobering but hopeful journey about how one young German boy copes with the war and propaganda. Based on true events.

A Piece of Blue String (companion short story)

THE CLOCKWISE COLLECTION (YA time travel romance)

Casey Donovan has issues: hair, height and uncontrollable trips to the 19th century! And now this ~ she's accidentally taken Nate Mackenzie, the cutest boy in the school, back in time. Awkward.

Clockwise

Clockwiser

Like Clockwork

Counter Clockwise

Clockwork Crazy

Clocked (companion novella)

<u>Standalones</u>

Seaweed

Love, Tink

ABOUT THE AUTHOR

Lee Strauss is a USA TODAY bestselling author of The Ginger Gold Mysteries series, The Higgins & Hawke Mystery series, The Rosa Reed Mystery series (cozy historical mysteries), A Nursery Rhyme Mystery series (mystery suspense), The Perception series (young adult dystopian), The Light & Love series (sweet romance), The Clockwise Collection (YA time travel romance), and young adult historical fiction with over a million books read. She has titles published in German, Spanish and Korean, and a growing audio library.

When Lee's not writing or reading she likes to cycle, hike, and stare at the ocean. She loves to drink caffè lattes and red wines in exotic places, and eat dark chocolate anywhere.

For more info on books by Lee Strauss and her social media links, visit leestraussbooks.com. To make sure you don't miss the next new release, be sure to sign up for her readers' list!

Discuss the books, ask questions, share your opinions.

Fun giveaways! Join the Lee Strauss Readers' Group on Facebook for more info.

Love the fashions of the 1920s? Check out Ginger Gold's Pinterest Board!

Did you know you can follow your favourite authors on Bookbub? If you subscribe to Bookbub — (and if you don't, why don't you? - They'll send you daily emails alerting you to sales and new releases on just the kind of books you like to read!) — follow me to make sure you don't miss the next Ginger Gold Mystery!

www.leestraussbooks.com

leestraussbooks@gmail.com

facebook.com/AuthorLeeStrauss

twitter.com/LeeStraussBooks
instagram.com/lee.strauss

CPSIA information can be obtained
at www.ICGtesting.com
Printed in the USA
BVHW051657150722
642242BV00005B/218